PINE

INTERGALACTIC DATING AGENCY

DRAGON BRIDES
BOOK TEN

KATE RUDOLPH

ABOUT PINE

The holidays are coming and all Neve can say is bah humbug.

When she wins an all expenses paid trip to a winter wonderland, she's ready to leave her life behind for relaxation without Christmas trees and elves. The last thing she expects is to land on an alien planet and meet a dragon lord.

Lord Pine needs an escort to the king's Yule Ball. But he's not looking for a bride, and all the dragon ladies of Vemion are sure to have expectations. Enter the Intergalactic Dating Agency. All he needs is a date, but Neve is more than he could have hoped for.

But every holiday comes to an end. Pine will need to win his human over - and convince her this isn't a dream - or he'll lose his mate forever.

1

By order of His Majesty King Venin of Vemion, you are cordially invited to the Royal Yule Celebration.

The vellum was thick in Pine's hand, and he might have crumpled it up if the messenger wasn't standing right there awaiting a response. One didn't make the king wait to fill out his guest list.

"I would be honored to attend." The words came out even. He couldn't manage happy, not when he wanted to scream or cry or rage that his father's ashes were barely scattered.

He was head of his family now, a dragon lord in truth. Insulting the king would do him no good.

Besides, he could always plead an illness and

cancel at the last moment. The king could hardly hold it against him if he had dragon mumps.

The messenger bowed and retreated from his office, heading for the front door, no doubt on his way to deliver even more holiday tidings of doom.

The king loves to meddle.

He could hear the words in his father's raspy voice, the fond smile on his face only possible since he'd played politics for more than eighty years. He'd lived for the cutthroat life of the dragon court. Pine had always felt like a fool, a prize on display who's only job was to not disappoint his father.

He'd succeeded. So why did he still feel like *this*?

He set the invitation down on his desk and glanced at the framed photo of him, his father, and his sister at some function or another when Briar still had the gangly proportions of a growing girl. It had been the three of them since his mother left, unable to handle court life or anything else on Vemion. He hadn't heard from her in seventeen years.

Should he tell her that her former husband was dead? Was she even still alive?

It was another duty to add to the growing pile.

Happy, heavy footsteps pounded down the

plushly carpeted hall outside of his office, and his sister burst into the room, face bright with excitement and her auburn in a swirl of curls and tangles around her face.

"Was that the king's messenger?" she demanded, throwing herself into a chair, letting her legs hang over the side. She was wearing breeches and smelled of the stables.

What use did a girl have for a horse when her other form was a dragon?

Not a girl, he reminded himself. A young woman. And equally summoned.

He pinched the corner of the invitation with two fingers, as if it might burn him, and gingerly handed it over.

She vibrated with excitement as she read, shifting in her chair and leaning forward, placing the invitation back on the desk and smiling like a madwoman. "The king's Yule ball? This is amazing!"

"I'm not so sure about that." Ever since the king had married off his three sons, he'd been in a matrimonial mood, wanting all of the young lords and ladies paired up and creating even more little lordlings.

This would be the first year without their father.

While Briar might want the distraction, Pine feared he'd be no good to anyone. It was far better to beg off than to disappoint the king in person.

"We *have* to go." Briar shot out of her chair and placed both of her hands on his desk, planting herself in a familiar, stubborn stance. "It's supposed to be the event of the season. Everyone who's anyone will be there. And this *will* help me get a job in the ministry. You said you wanted that, didn't you?"

At nineteen, Briar could have been doing anything. Or nothing. She was a lady, wealthy, and had energy to spare. And Pine knew that energy would be put to no good use if she didn't have some sort of outlet.

"That's already in the works," he reminded her. "I've spoken with a friend from the academy. He'll invite you to an interview after the holidays. No party needed."

She pursed her lips. "Father would want us to go."

It landed like a fireball between them.

She was right. She knew that he knew she was right. And Pine couldn't help but scowl and stick his tongue out at her, a wisp of smoke escaping with it.

"That's not playing fair." He had a stack of papers a dragon high and had to sort through everything his father had left behind. Despite his age, the man hadn't expected to pass so soon, and now it was Pine's problem.

"Playing fair never gets you what you want." Briar had a look on her face that said she knew she had won.

Pine groaned. "Go terrorize someone else, brat."

She laughed and retreated out of the room, leaving him to consider his options.

It was one thing to beg off to the king. To his sister? Never. He was going to the Yule Ball.

And that was how he found himself in a comfortable room in a discreet storefront waiting for a woman who was rumored to be the best matchmaker in all of Vemion. Not that Pine wanted the best. Maybe he should have just put out an advert: *Date needed for royal ball. Strictly business.*

A woman in a diaphanous blue skirt and silk top came in and poured herself a cup of tea before she took a seat opposite him on the sofa. "I'm Shade," she said. "Welcome."

He got right to it. Shade seemed ready to make small talk, and that was the last thing Pine needed. "I need to escort someone to the Yule Ball. I am not looking for love, or a wife, or anything of the sort. Can you help me?"

The matchmaker sipped her tea before placing the cup in its saucer. "That's not something I do."

He could taste acrid smoke in his mouth and breathed deep to pull it back. He was an adult dragon; he wouldn't smoke up the place like an undisciplined youth. "If payment is—"

"Your lordship, *that* is not a service I offer." She reared back as if struck.

"I'm not asking for a ... lady of pleasure." He stumbled over the words. Hiring a prostitute to pose as his date had never occurred to him. Should it have? "I thought that, perhaps, you would know a lady that would like to attend the Yule Ball with no expectations. Or promises. Or hopes."

Shade settled back down, but her expression was still skeptical. "The ladies I work with all have hopes and expectations, my lord. I am not in the business of ... temporary arrangements." He was about to get up and figure something else out when she held up a hand. "But I'm intrigued. Why did you come to me?"

Because he was a fool. But that wouldn't do for an excuse.

"Your name has become known after the recent

matches you orchestrated. It seems that every dragon prince or lord that crosses your path finds his mate. Which is *not* what I'm looking for. I'm dealing with the fallout from my father's death. Our estate is a mess, and it will take time and dedication to fix it. Time I cannot offer a new bride. I know that the king has been in a matrimony minded mood ever since his sons all married. I do not want to walk into the Yule Ball as a newly elevated lord with a space at my side for a lady. If the king were to command me to find a bride, I could not refuse to try." He hadn't meant to say all of that, but Shade sat and listened, nodding along so compassionately that he couldn't stop talking.

"Is it that you're not inclined to a bride? Are you looking for a groom? Because I can arrange that as well."

"I'm not looking for anyone." He needed that to be clear. "When it's time to wed, I'm sure I can find a woman on my own. No offense."

"Hmm." Shade steepled her fingers together and narrowed her eyes. "You come to my business, ask me to perform a service I do not offer, and insult the one I do. You need to learn better manners, lordship."

He huffed out a laugh. "So we agree that I'm not ready for a wife."

Shade thought for a moment before finally nodding. "I can find you someone. The king seems fond of humans. What do you think?"

"Anyone will do." It was just one night.

How bad could it be?

2

Neve glared at the holiday display at the entrance to the store. The blinking, colorful lights were probably going fast enough to give someone a seizure. And was it close enough to block the exit in case of a fire? The fire marshal might want to look into it.

Bah humbug.

Though her fingers twitched to put in the complaint, she forced herself to do her shopping and leave the store without spreading her holiday misery to everyone else.

Christmas sucked.

Her parents were no doubt in the middle of planning the big holiday bash, the guest list ranging from the mayor to every minor celebrity in the tri-town area. That mostly meant one reality show wannabe who got kicked off their dating show after three episodes and a perennial national athlete who never quite made it to the finals.

Neve wouldn't be there. She hadn't bothered to RSVP. Last year she'd forced herself to put on a sparkly dress, paste a smile on her face, and play nice. She hadn't even seen her parents the entire night.

No use wasting time this year.

She passed by houses decked out in enough lights to be a fire hazard and pulled into her own driveway where the only light was the security floodlight above the back door. Neve grabbed her mail and shouldered her way through the door, her hands burdened with envelopes and groceries.

She needed a vacation.

But there were chores to be done, and Neve didn't let herself collapse onto the couch until the food was put away and she'd dealt with the dishes that had been sitting in the sink for two days.

Finally seated, she flipped through the mail. Junk. Junk. Bill. Junk. Ju—what?

At first, she thought the embossed envelope had to be a scam. But something made her open it and pull out the finely printed card inside.

YOU'VE WON AN ALL EXPENSES PAID WINTER GETAWAY!

That couldn't be right. The last time she'd tried to win a contest was for concert tickets off the radio back in high school. But Neve kept reading. The card looked legit. But it couldn't be. People didn't just win random contests they didn't enter.

It nagged at her the rest of the day, and after a while, she finally went online and started digging. Someone would confirm it was a well-known scam, and then she'd be satisfied.

Except the opposite happened.

There were social media posts and articles and websites all confirming that the company behind the contest: IDA Worlds Travel was legit, even if it sounded like a typo. And the contest had been happening for years.

Could Neve have entered without remembering? Maybe it was some sort of credit card benefit?

She looked at the card again, and before she could give it a second thought, called the number.

Two days later, she was on a private plane.

It was a whirlwind, and it still didn't feel real, but Neve had decided to go along for the ride. This way, there'd be not temptation to go to her parents' holiday party. There'd be no guilt about not putting up a single decoration or pretending she cared about the holidays. She was going to a snow-capped resort where she would care about nothing but relaxation and rest for an entire week.

Paradise.

At some point, Neve fell asleep. It was strange. She was never able to sleep on planes. But maybe that had to do with being cramped between people who hogged the arm rest and reclined their chairs so she was wedged in with barely enough space to breathe.

She woke with a jolt and was disoriented for a moment, her ears popping and head going fuzzy.

Where was she?

On the plane. Right. Headed for a winter paradise.

She realized they weren't flying anymore when the flight attendant greeted her with a smile and urged her off the plane and ushered her into somewhere that definitely wasn't an airport.

Damn it. This had always been too good to be true.

Was she being kidnapped? What kind of kidnappers used a private plane for just one person? That couldn't be financially feasible.

Neve was panicking. She could feel it in the

shape of her thoughts. Who had time to care about criminal finances when they had to run?

The flight attendant had disappeared, probably off to do some nefarious task. She was in a huge empty room, the walls a dark gray, light coming in through a large opening in the ceiling. There were no signs, nothing telling her where to go. And she didn't see a door.

She needed to get out of there. Wherever *there* was.

"Ah, you made it." A man's voice cut through her panic like a warm breeze on a cold day. "I hope your trip was comfortable." He had a slight accent, something she couldn't place.

She turned around and had to stop in her tracks.

Damn.

He was hot.

Hotter than hot.

Dark hair, cut short, with a slight curl that made her want to run her hands through it. Piercing green eyes. Broad shoulders. A chest that stretched the fabric of his white button up shirt.

If this was a kidnapper, maybe she didn't need to be too eager to run away.

"Who are you? Where am I?" It came out desperate, but she sounded more angry than scared. Angry was good. She could use that.

The man placed his hand on his chest and gave a shallow bow. "Of course, my apologies. My name is P—" he cleared his throat, "Lord Pine, and we're at my hangar on Vemion. I'm so glad you've agreed to all this. I hear it's difficult to find humans who know about dragons and are willing to leave their planet. I hope this will be a pleasant experience for the both of us."

Dragons.

Planet.

What?

Neve's mouth fell open, and she tried to speak, but she couldn't think of a single word worth saying.

The nervous breakdown that had been chasing her all season had finally caught up.

3

There had clearly been a miscommunication somewhere.

The human, Neve, had been muttering to herself for several minutes as Pine directed her to the transport vehicle and drove them up to the manor. He thought he'd been clear with the matchmaker. She had suggested a human, but why would she send one with no knowledge of dragons?

"This can't be real." Neve gasped, and Pine followed her gaze to see an unfamiliar looping through the sky in the distance. "It's fake."

He had to fix this.

Fast.

The Yule Ball was coming up soon, and there

wasn't time for the matchmaker to find him another human. It shouldn't matter. If he had a speck of decency, he'd turn the transport around and take Neve back to the hangar to send her home so that she could pretend this whole thing had never happened.

But decency was hard to cling to when he was desperate.

He turned the transport down a path away from the manor and towards the cliffs that bordered the lake on the edge of the estate. This human didn't believe in dragons? It was time to see if an example might be enough to snap her out of her daze.

They came to a stop, and Neve jolted. "What's going on? Where are we?" She sprang out of her side of the transport. There were no doors, and he hadn't thought to mention the safety restraint she should have had buckled over her hips. "What do you want with me?" She had her hands up, whether to ward off an attack or jab out a punch, he wasn't sure.

He kept his distance all the same.

Pine undid his safety restraint and powered down the transport before slowly walking around until he was closer to Neve, but still several feet away. "I'm sorry that we got off on the wrong foot. I thought I would ... well, perhaps a demonstration is for the best."

He turned around and started sprinting. Neve yelled after him, but her words were swallowed by the wind.

Pine launched himself off the edge of the cliff and let the transformation take him over, body shifting and expanding from one form to the other in the blink of an eye. He spread out his blue wings and let the wind take him, soaring out over the lake and flying higher and higher until Neve was little more than a speck on the ground.

He let out a burst of fire, more to show off than anything else.

Joy lifted him even higher, his worries and grief falling down to the surface. There was nothing but the simplicity and complexity of flight up here. He wasn't carrying the mantle of a new title. He wasn't missing a father taken too soon. He wasn't concerned at whatever the future held for his sister.

He was just a dragon riding the wind.

He glided down slowly, circling around and around, catching site of Neve, who seemed to be mirroring his circles, her eyes never leaving his form. He shifted again, landing on two feet as a man just to see the shock on her face. He couldn't have stopped the grin that pulled at his lips if he tried.

"What do you think?"

Neve's mouth was hanging open, and she had to close it to gulp. He could see her throat working as she processed what she'd seen. "That's impossible."

"Not here." He gestured around. "You're on Vemion now, a planet ruled by dragons."

Her tongue darted out to lick her lips. "Can I see you again?"

Neve had gone off the deep end, and for some reason she wasn't desperately reaching for a life preserver. If this was going crazy, at least it was the coolest thing she'd ever seen.

She could worry about sanity later.

Pine's lips quirked up into a gentle smile, something that made a funny clench in her chest. Oh no. It was one thing to believe the guy could impossibly change from man to dragon, it was something completely else to be attracted to him. She would only allow her break with reality to go so far.

Instead of jumping off a cliff and trying to give her another heart attack, Pine took a few steps back, breathed deep, and the air around him shimmered for an instant before a giant blue beast stood before her.

She let out a breath and reached out a hand, her fingers trembling. The dragon lowered its head, and Neve touched the smooth scales, the heat of it making her gasp.

It felt so real. Like it couldn't be a dream.

But it had to be fake.

His blue scales shimmered in the sunlight, dragging her eyes towards the massive wings that he held tight to his body.

"I'm losing my mind," she whispered.

Then he lowered one wing, and she could swear she heard a voice in her head saying *might as well go for a ride*. It sounded like a stray thought, not like someone was trying to talk to her. And it sounded like Pine's voice.

More proof she was crazy.

But if this wasn't real, shouldn't she enjoy it?

Neve climbed his wing carefully, marveling at just how real it all felt. Scales and muscle moved under her feet, and it was an unsteady climb to the center of his back. He moved under her, and she nearly fell before finding her seat and clutching at a lump of scaly skin at the top of his back.

She never drove her car without a seat belt. This? This was going to get her killed.

But before she could call it off and jump for safety, Pine moved. There were none of the tricks she'd seen him pull a few minutes ago. Now he just walked gently towards the cliff and started pumping his wings, lifting off from the ground and soaring like it was nothing.

Neve pressed herself flat to his back and clenched her legs, hoping for more grip, the whole of his body unsteady under her.

Wind butted her face, her hair whipping around her and trying to lash her but only getting caught in her mouth.

This was real. It was all too real.

Neve screamed.

But somewhere in the middle of the desperate cry, it turned to laughter. How had this happened to her? She'd known it was impossible to win some winter getaway, but never could have imagined ending up on another *planet*. And yet, there she was. There was no way anyone could demand she go to her parents' vapid party if she wasn't even in the same *solar system*.

By the time Pine landed, she couldn't stop smiling.

This was the craziest thing that would ever happen to her. She had no idea how it was even possible. But it was as real as the bills piling up in her mailbox back home.

She'd just ridden a dragon.

She was on an alien planet.

She was going to enjoy it.

Scrambling off Pine's back was just as tricky as getting on, and she could already tell just how much her muscles were going to hurt in a day or two. It might have seemed like she was sitting still, but riding a dragon was a workout.

Pine shifted back to his human form, and he was smiling just as broadly as she was. "Thank you," he said.

"Thank *me*? Why?" She tried combing her hair back into some semblance of order with her fingers but found they were shaking. She balled them into fists to try and tamp down the adrenaline.

"I had forgotten how fun it can be to just fly for the joy of it. I have been busy these last few months." The smile slid away, and whatever worries he was facing seemed to come back.

Neve wasn't sure what to say to that. "Why did you bring me here, Pine—should I call you Lord Pine? What's that all about?" The closest she'd come to any kind of lord was watching that show on Netflix. She was pretty sure it didn't count.

"Just Pine will do." He nodded towards the golf cart looking vehicle they'd ridden in. "Come, I'll explain as we drive to the house."

"How can I even understand you?" She wasn't going to question the evolution of it all. That was way too much for her fragile brain to handle at the moment. But even if two human-like species had managed to evolve on totally separate planets, there was no way they'd both developed English as a language.

Pine gestured behind his ear. "Feel around there. You should have been outfitted with a translator."

She did as instructed and felt several bumps right behind her ear. Touching them tickled, and she flinched, pulling her hand away. "How? This can't be real."

But it was.

They climbed back into the dragon golf cart, and Pine started driving. "You were brought here by the Intergalactic Dating Agency," he said out of nowhere.

"The what-ting agency?" Sure, she'd been on Tinder, but there hadn't been any dragons that she remembered.

"I'm not looking for a bride, I assure you."

"So you flew me a bajillion light years away to tell me you don't want to date? Do they not have texting on your planet?" Not that she wanted to date *him*, but no girl liked getting rejected.

"I'm not explaining this properly. King Venin is throwing his annual Yule Ball soon. I have just risen to my father's title, and as new head of the family must attend. The king is often in a matchmaking mood, and that is one complication I am hoping to avoid. So I asked the Royal Matchmaker to find me a date. That's where you come in."

Neve opened her mouth but couldn't find the right words to ask him why there were no eligible women on his own planet.

He took her silence as an invitation to keep speaking. "The party is nonsense, simply a time for the king to show off and the lords and ladies to dance around and be seen. I simply need to cement my position ... Are you alright?"

She was frowning. She'd fled one vapid Christmas party and landed on a whole other planet, invited to one that was even worse. "Surely there was some woman on Vemion who could go? You didn't have to take me."

"I am sorry for that. Shade was not exactly clear

on the process. I thought you would know all about this. Once the ball is done, I promise to send you home in the height of luxury. Don't you want to see how dragons party?"

It was a once-in-a-lifetime opportunity. Today was already an impossible day.

And what choice did she really have? She didn't know how to get home, and she doubted any space-ship she found would take Visa.

They crested a hill, and a giant manor house came into view.

Lord Pine was loaded.

But was he as good as his word?

"When's the party? I can't wait."

4

It was a whirlwind of a first day, but when Neve begged off with a headache and a need for a shower, Pine let her go. Her room was something out of a fairytale, or a hotel way too high end for her to ever afford. But compared to flying on the back of a dragon, it was nothing.

The next morning, she tried to tell herself she wasn't hiding. No one had told her if breakfast was at a certain time or if there was some sort of schedule. Was the party that day? How long was she supposed to stay on this dragon planet?

She really hadn't asked enough questions the day before.

Neve told her brain to give the rest of her a break. It wasn't like she found out alien dragons existed every day. That kind of overwrote every other thing she might think about.

Did she even have appropriate clothing? She'd packed for a winter getaway and had thrown in a little black dress at the last moment. But it certainly wasn't something she'd wear to a ball.

There was a large wardrobe standing like a soldier against one wall. Neve opened it, hoping that maybe clothes had materialized overnight for her to wear, but there was nothing. And when she checked the back wall of the wardrobe, it was solid. No portal to another world. If there was one, she would hope it took her back to Earth.

"You've gone off the deep end," she muttered to herself.

Excited knocking at the door made her jolt in surprise, and before she could answer, the door creaked open, and a young woman with red hair and a broad smile on her face slipped in. "Do you mind if I come in? How'd you sleep?" She was bouncing from foot to foot, energy eager to burst out of her.

Was this another dragon? Was everyone but her a dragon?

Neve stared at the girl, not quite able to get her mind around what she was supposed to say. Where was Pine? At least she knew him.

Sort of.

"I'm Briar," said the young woman. "Pine's my brother. I'm so happy you agreed to this whole thing. I know it's kind of ridiculous and all, but Pine never just has fun with stuff, you know? Have the servants sent up breakfast? Are you hungry? Are you ready?" The questions poured out of her mouth like a landslide.

A younger sister. Apparently they were the same on every planet. Neve didn't have siblings herself, but she knew the type. "I haven't eaten." That was a good place to start. "And ready for what?"

Briar practically skipped into the room and looped her arm into Neve's. "Come on."

Breakfast was a relatively simple affair of fruits she didn't recognize and bread with cheese and some kind of meat. She didn't ask questions. They wouldn't serve her humans, right? Did dragons eat humans? Was she doing cannibalism?

Even though the meat was tender and well-seasoned, Neve avoided the rest of it and finished the fruit, bread, and cheese. It was another thing she couldn't think too hard about.

A servant walked into the room just as Neve was finishing her juice and addressed Briar. "The modiste is here, my lady."

"Thank you, Rendell." Briar grinned at her. "Pine doesn't think of this stuff. Come on, let's get you ready!"

And that was how Neve found herself standing in front of hastily set up mirrors in a sitting room, with cloth draped over her as Briar and the modiste, Kerren, eyed her like she was some sort of moving doll.

"What's going on?" Pine's voice startled her, and Neve jerked, brushing against a few of the pins keeping all the cloth in place.

"What do you think?" Briar asked, hovering her hands over Neve as she showed off the icy blue fabric.

Pine's eyes raked her from head to toe, and the heat of it felt strong enough to melt the icicle blue of her dress. Neve met his eyes defiantly. He'd gotten her into this mess, and he had to see it through.

They stared at one another for a heavy second. There was green in his eyes, flecks of it offset by gray. How strange. And pretty.

She didn't often think a man had pretty eyes.

Maybe it was the eyelashes. They were long and thick and framed his eyes like a painting.

Pine cleared his throat and looked back at the

framework of a dress she was wearing. "You'll probably want to sew it all together before the ball."

Briar groaned. "You have no taste. Begone, dragon man." She shooed him with a negligent wave.

Pine chuckled and left them alone.

"He's really not so bad," Briar said once he was probably out of earshot. "He just takes too much on. He's got the weight of the world on his shoulders."

Neve would be lying if she said she wasn't curious. This was a man who'd summoned a woman from another planet for a simple date. In her experience, people who did things like that, or at least the Earth equivalent, weren't worried about how their actions affected others. "Is that so?"

"He's worried that if he doesn't make a good impression then I won't get the job I want in the ministry. The king seemed nice enough when I was presented at court, but Pine is always thinking about the ways things can go wrong. I hope he actually has fun at this ball. He hasn't since Father died."

He'd said something about that, hadn't he? Or something about newly ascending to his title. Neve kept her mouth shut. Briar wanted to talk, and it couldn't hurt to learn more about what was going on.

"Father was quite old when I was born, but he did everything he could for us. He got sick last year and just ... faded. I don't think Pine let himself see it coming. And because Father was sick for so long, there's issues with the estate. Nothing that we can't handle, you understand, but it's a lot of work at once. And now with the king forcing him to go to the ball ..."

"I thought you said he wanted to go because of your job." Briar had said a lot, and Neve wasn't sure if it all connected.

"When the king invites you to something like this, you don't get to say no unless you can come up with a really good excuse. Pine thought he could get away with just saying he was sick. I convinced him otherwise. So I guess you have me to thank for this whole thing. What do you think about beading around the collar?"

Neve's mind reeled there. Was Pine as bad as her parents, putting on a big show at the holidays merely for clout and position, or was it something more? Did it even matter? She was only going to be there until the ball; she didn't need to get caught up in family squabbles.

The modiste made some adjustments, and suddenly there was a string of delicate glass beads along Neve's collar and the draping almost truly looked like a dress. "I have enough here, ma'am. I can have this back to you the morning of the ball. That's three days. If there are final fit adjustments, we'll have to do them then."

Briar sighed but didn't argue.

Neve put her clothes on as the modiste packed up the fabric and supplies. At some point, Briar slipped from the room, and once the modiste left, Neve was alone.

What now?

She had no idea what time it was or if they even kept time like on Earth. Was lunch a thing on Vemion? And what else did Pine—or was it Briar— have in store for her today?

The door opened again, and Pine stepped in. "Did all go well with the dressmaker?"

"I hope so. I guess we'll know before the party." At least she knew what to expect for her parents' Christmas shindig. She was flying blind here. "So what can I expect? Dragons flying around all night? Fireworks?" Human sacrifice? She kept the last one to herself.

Pine took a step closer. "There will be food. Music. Dancing. The king will say a few words. It's all ..." He sighed and didn't finish the sentence.

He wanted to go to this ball about as much as she wanted to attend her parents' Christmas party, except no one was about to kidnap him and secret him away to another planet. Maybe the dress fitting had put her in a good mood or at least cemented that there was no getting out of the event, but Neve wanted to cheer him up. She couldn't banish his grief, but at least she could help him have a pleasant night.

"What kind of dancing do dragons get up to?" She shimmied her hips to music only she could hear and moved her hands up and down.

"What's *that*?" Pine was horrified.

"It's disco! Saturday Night Fever, baby." She laughed at his horror and started to do the running man and any other silly move she could think of.

"Is this what passes for dancing on your planet?"

Normally, you couldn't see a person question every life choice that led to this individual moment, but right then Neve could, and it made her laugh even harder.

"Why don't you show me what they'll expect? Unless you want me to show you how to boogie." Even saying it made her feel like she was living in some movie from the seventies, but Pine's sour mood seemed to be getting sweeter with every one of her antics.

He pulled something that looked like a regular phone out of his pocket and played with the screen for a moment until a melody started to play. It was like nothing she'd heard before on instruments she probably couldn't imagine, but it was beautiful. "Come here," he said and beckoned her forward.

Neve stepped close and realized her mistake.

Pine's scent enveloped her, something masculine and earthy with just a hint of spice. She wanted to roll around in it, bottle it up, and wear it forever. Her body lit up the closer they stood.

And she'd tempted him to dance.

This was a bad idea.

But she was only here for a few days. What would it hurt if she flirted a bit? After the party, she'd go home carrying impossible memories, things she could never tell anyone else if she hoped to be believed. She could flirt with a dragon.

She could do more than flirt.

"Show me how dragons dance."

Pine put a hand on her waist and drew her close, their bodies pressing together as he guided her in a slow and simple rhythm.

Neve could feel the heat of him, his muscles moving beneath his clothes, and his breath tickling her neck. She shivered and clung to him, not knowing what she was doing but trusting him to lead her through it.

It was the simplest of moves, but somehow the most sensual.

She never wanted it to end.

But Pine pulled back and smiled down at her, his eyes hooded. "That's something simple. I think you pull it off well."

"What's something hard?" The words felt completely filthy on her tongue, but maybe the double meaning didn't translate properly.

Pine put both of his hands on her hips and moved again. It was a more intense step this time, the music pounding out a beat she could barely match. She tried to follow Pine's footwork, but after a few seconds tripped, and he had to catch her, turning it into a perfectly executed dip.

The man could dance.

He helped her back up but didn't let go.

Neve didn't step back.

Her eyes flicked down to his lips, and her tongue darted out to wet her own. If she was ever going to seize the moment, the time was now.

She leaned in and brushed her lips against his. It was gentle. An invitation.

She pulled back and met Pine's eyes, waiting to see what he might do next.

She thought she smelled smoke.

Any worry evaporated as he leaned in and captured her lips with his own. His kiss was hot and urgent, like they were more than strangers, like he was a man dying of thirst, and she was his water.

It was all Neve could do to keep up, clinging to his shoulders and letting him take the lead. He groaned against her mouth, his hand cupping her ass and keeping her pressed tight to him.

She could feel him.

All of him.

And she wanted more.

But Pine pulled away, practically throwing her out of his embrace as he backed away. He swiped his hand against his mouth, and there was a strange halo of smoke that seemed to gather around his legs.

It must have been a dragon thing.

"I think you'll manage to dance just fine. Excuse me, I have to go."

And he fled.

5

The dress fit. It flowed around her and clung in all the right places when she spun around and made her feel just a little bit like a princess.

Pine was looking at her like she was something out of a fairy tale. His mouth hung slightly open, and his eyes blazed with an impossible light. Then he shook his head a little, and the expression was gone as if it had never been there at all.

But Neve had definitely seen it.

Her lips tingled in memory of their kiss, and she tried to banish the thought. In the days since then, she'd barely seen Pine and had, instead, been ferried around by his sister, who showed her everything the estate had to offer.

It didn't matter that she was a bit disappointed not to spend time with the dragon who could light her up from inside with one kiss. After tonight, she'd be going home. That was good. She could hold these memories close until they started to fade into nothing but a pleasant thought she wasn't sure was real or a dream. No need to dwell on the less than perfect parts.

Pine offered his arm and lead her to the entryway of the manor where Briar was waiting in a similarly elegant gown, her hair done up in a complicated style with a large ornament sticking out from the back of her head that looked a bit like a hand fan painted with an intricate design.

Neve's hair was gently styled, a bit of curling, a bit of the dragon equivalent of hairspray, and it hung down past her shoulders. Simple and elegant. But she felt understlyed next to Briar.

"You look amazing!" Briar said. "I knew the dress would be perfect. Everyone's going to want to see you. Especially since they've been hearing rumors about the human that Pine's been keeping to himself."

"Briar!" A puff of smoke burst out of Pine's mouth, and he glared. "You know this isn't real. She'll be gone after tonight. What are you doing?"

This isn't real.

It echoed in Neve's mind. Of course it wasn't. She'd spent maybe a half an hour alone with Pine since she got here, and most of that had been spent arguing.

Or kissing.

But the kissing was irrelevant. Pine didn't want her. He didn't want anyone. And she wasn't here to fall in love with a strange dragon man. She had a life back on Earth, and she had to make it through tonight to get back there.

Briar was unrepentant. "You'll thank me later."

Before things could erupt into a sibling blowout, a servant cleared his throat and announced that their carriage was ready.

This was a different vehicle than the one Pine had used to drive her around the property earlier. There was still something vaguely golf cart-ish to the shape of it, but it was like a golf cart and a carriage out of a fairy tale had a baby. Gold and silver weaved together to form the walls of the traveling compartment, and a driver sat at the front in a simple but finely decorated area all to himself.

A door on the side slid open, and a set of stairs automatically descended. Briar was first into the carriage, followed by Neve. Pine took her hand and assist her in before following.

She didn't dare look at him. He was just being polite. Probably acting on instinct and nothing more.

There were two padded benches facing each other in the cabin. Pine sat beside Neve, their legs pressed together.

Again, nothing to read into it. He just didn't want to be crammed in next to his sister.

The carriage drove them towards the city and the castle on the hill in the middle of it. Neve couldn't bring herself to do more than glance out the windows once or twice. She'd be leaving tomorrow. She didn't want to see something in town she'd regret not having visited. Better not to know than to miss it forever.

Briar had no such compunction. She was looking outside like she'd never seen the city before and kept saying things like "we need to go to that bakery next week" or "did you see the new bookshop? Why didn't you tell me?"

Neve didn't respond. Briar and her brother could do whatever they wanted next week. There were bakeries and bookstores on Earth. Neve wasn't really missing out.

The carriage slowed to a crawl as they joined the line of attendees for the king's Yule Ball.

Briar sat for several moments, energy thrumming under her skin and barely contained. Then she reached for the latch on the door. "You guys can wait. I'm walking the rest of the way." She was out of the car before either Neve or Pine could reach to stop her.

Pine knocked his head against the headrest. "I have no idea where she gets the energy."

It was a little exhausting just watching her, but Neve didn't say it out loud. "Is walking to the entrance a faux pas?" They'd been in the line of carriages for about ten minutes and had only moved a few dozen feet.

"Not when it's Briar. She'll charm anyone she meets and probably be leading a brigade of attendees with muddy shoes to be announced as one group. The king's lucky she has no desire to rule. I dread to think what kind of revolution she'd lead." He turned towards her with a faint smile. "I hope you don't mind waiting until we arrive at the entrance."

"No problem." Neve looked right back at him and felt an answering smile threatening to tug at her lips. That way lay danger. And monsters. And bottomless pits of despair.

She forced herself to look away.

If there had been an opportunity there, it vanished as the silence between them dragged on. Neve wished she knew what to say, but every moment was a reminder that she was that much closer to home, and there was no need to start anything; she couldn't finish it.

If Pine had let that kiss draw to its natural conclusion three days ago, it would be a different story. But he'd run away. She refused to put herself out there again.

Finally, the carriage pulled up to the entrance, and Pine exited first, putting out a hand to help her down the steps.

Despite what he'd said, the way was paved with gleaming marble stones that seemed to have flecks of gold in them. The entrance was an archway out of a fantasy novel's dream, gold weaved together to look like tree branches. None of the other people getting out of their carriages paid the entrance any mind.

She was surrounded by dragons. This was real.

Neve stopped gawking. It was time to do her job.

She pasted on a smile and put her hand in the

crook of Pine's arm, letting him lead her in. A few moments later, they were announced by a man in a fine black robe who stood at the other end of the golden archway. Some curious attendees looked their way, but not many. Hopefully Briar's promise of curious dragons was an empty threat.

The inside of the palace was no less ornate than the outside. It reminded her a little of Versailles, which she'd gone to on a school trip her senior year of high school. Four years of French class had finally paid off. Not because she could actually speak it, because she really couldn't, but the sights had been amazing.

Apparently the dragon king didn't know what all that opulence had done for King Louis. But she didn't see hoards of angry peasants armed with a guillotine, so maybe things were going alright here.

"What are you thinking about?" Pine asked as he led her farther into the ballroom.

"Um ... monarchy?" Now was not the time to talk about the French Revolution. She needed to remember why she was here. "Any special instructions? Are we trying to impress anyone? Or do you just need me to keep my mouth shut, smile, and look pretty?"

"Do what you wish with your mouth; you're

beautiful enough as it is." He seemed to realize what he said only after the words came out, and his eyes widened.

Neve couldn't help it. She laughed.

Somewhere, musicians were tuning their instruments, and attendees began to line up in a formation that Neve recognized from her dancing lessons. Pine held out a hand, and they joined them.

Then the music started, and she let her worries float away.

She was going to have fun, and then she was going to go home.

6

If Pine kept staring at Neve like he was, people would truly believe he'd brought her to Vemion to be his bride. But he couldn't look away. They'd danced through the first two songs like their bodies were made to move together.

For the third, Briar had cut in with a significant look. It was one thing to have a favored partner, but dancing with only one woman was almost scandalous.

Another dragon had snatched Neve up, and the night had moved on.

Something curdled in Pine's stomach as he watched the human dance with a dragon named Cipher. A nephew of the king, if he recalled, and happily mated to a human. That didn't make Pine feel any better.

"Pine? I'd heard you accepted Father's invitation, but I didn't believe it." Prince Crux, son and heir of King Venin wore all the regalia of his station and grinned as if he didn't have a care in the world.

"I wouldn't miss it," he lied. They'd attended for a couple of hours already, but the king had yet to make an appearance. Once he did, Pine would make sure he was seen, and then they could go.

Crux coughed, and it might have been to cover a laugh. "I hear you brought a human. I didn't know you were looking for a mate. The IDA?"

Pine clamped down on the instinctive denial. The entire point of this endeavor was so that he wouldn't be matched with a stranger. Tomorrow, Neve would go home, and he could tell anyone who asked that it hadn't worked out. He needed to redirect this conversation. "Where is your human? I haven't seen Lady Courtney."

It had caused a scandal when Crux declared the human Courtney as his mate. The scandal deepened when his brother Ranger had found a human of his own. Prince Saber had settled down with a proper dragon lady, but they didn't attend many royal events these days.

"My wife is unfortunately ill tonight. As soon as I see my father and give him my regards, I'll be heading home."

Fanfare played, and the room went silent between one breath and the next. King Venin walked through an archway adorned with flowers, and the whole room bowed to him. There was a beat as the attendees waited for the king to speak, but he just waved his hand and grabbed a glass of wine as the party resumed around him.

"That's my cue," said Crux.

"Send my regards to your wife," Pine said as the prince stalked off to find his father.

It was another half hour later before Pine thought it appropriate to approach the king. He couldn't seem too eager to get out of there. But when he pushed through the crowd to the king's table, he found it empty except for some eager courtiers who were laughing and drinking around the king's empty seat.

He spotted the king on the dance floor.

With Neve in his arms.

If she was nervous, she didn't show it. Her smile looked natural and made his heartbeat kick up. The king said something, and she laughed and said something back, though he couldn't tell what from this distance.

He wanted to cut in and rescue her but forced himself to stay still. The king had been nurturing a fascination with humans ever since his sons brought home their brides. That was the reason Pine had chosen Neve. He hadn't meant for her to have one on one time with His Majesty, but unless she said something egregious, she was in no danger.

What had she been thinking about monarchy earlier?

The song came to an end, and Neve gave a wobbly curtsy to the king.

Pine rushed towards her before another dragon could swoop in to claim the next dance. But before the music could start up, the king beckoned both him and Neve towards his table at the front of the room.

Neve clutched at his arm hard enough to leave bruises. She might look calm, but clearly it was an act.

"You've been hiding a gem, Lord Pine," said King Venin as he took his seat and picked up a glass of wine. "I did not know you'd sought a bride."

How did he contradict the king without actually telling the man he was wrong?

Neve saved him. "Oh, Your Majesty, we haven't gone that far yet." She smiled brightly. "Lord Pine and I are still in the early days of our courtship. I wouldn't want to rush."

The king nodded. "A sensible girl."

"Thank you, sir." She kept her gaze lowered.

Was this how humans treated their kings? It was strange, but it was working.

"I expect to see you both at my New Year's Ceremony in two weeks." He waved a hand, and a black-robed servant seemed to materialize out of nowhere. "Add Pine and his human to the guest list."

"What of his sister, Majesty?" the servant asked.

"Her, too, make it a family affair!" The king slung back his wine, and one of the courtiers refilled his glass.

Neve's fingers dug even harder into his arm.

But what was Pine supposed to say?

"It would be an honor, Your Majesty."

7

Neve kept the smile plastered to her face until the king dismissed them with a negligent wave. Pine put a guiding arm on her back, but she sashayed out of his grasp.

Don't make a scene.

Don't make a scene.

She wanted to scream.

Without looking or caring if he followed, she found an archway that led to a large balcony that circled the ballroom where several other partygoers had sneaked out to get fresh air.

"Neve—"

"What the hell?" She spun around at him as soon as they were out of earshot from the greater part of the ball. It would serve him right if she blew up at him in the middle of everyone, but she didn't want to be at the heart of the spectacle. "We had an agreement. I came to the party, I danced, I dazzled, I spoke highly of you to every man that twirled me around like I was a freaking ballerina. And now I'm supposed to go home. So what was *that*?" She jabbed her finger towards the door, vaguely in the direction of the king.

"What was I supposed to say?" Smoke swirled around him for a moment, quickly swallowed by the breeze.

"You could have pretended to *ask* me first!" Her hands were shaking, and she could feel angry tears threatening to fall, which only made her madder. This man, this dragon, didn't get to see her cry.

"And you would have said no to the king?"

"He's not my king." That was a little loud, and she took a deep breath before palace guards showed up to carry her off to the dungeons. "I have a life back on Earth. I don't want to stay here and be used by you."

"I'm not using you." Pine took a step forward, one hand reaching out.

Neve darted back. "That's the whole deal here. I played my part. You looked good. No one's going to try and find you a wife."

"I'm not using you," he repeated. There was a thread to his voice that sounded almost desperate. His eyes were pained; his whole face was. And he seemed to be unconsciously inching closer. They were in the middle of the balcony now, several steps from the hidden corner they'd started this argument in.

"Using me is the entire basis of this deal." Go to the party, play nice, go home. She'd done her part perfectly and ruined the holidays in the process.

Next year she was going somewhere they didn't have Christmas.

Like a deserted island.

"I know I asked you to stay for that purpose, but can't you feel something between us?" He was close enough to touch now, but Neve refused to give any more ground.

"You mean the one kiss we had where you ran away like my mouth was made of acid?" Not that she'd been dwelling on *that* at all.

"There's something here." He gestured between the two of them. "But I'm not holding you prisoner."

"So you'll get me that flight you promised?" It was a gauntlet thrown down.

Pine's jaw ticked. "Please consider staying. Not for the party. I don't care about that. Just—"

"I need a minute." And before he could grab onto her or say anything else that dripped with deception, Neve stalked away.

What in the name of all that was holy was Pine thinking? If Neve were a dragon, she'd be shooting fire right about now. She could almost feel the heat of it in her gut, a swirling bellows ready to rain death down on anyone who dared get too close.

She reined the fury back in. She was mad at Pine, not anyone else. Well, maybe the king, but being angry at kings never got a person anywhere good.

She wandered to the far side of the balcony and rested her elbows on the thick stone railing that ringed the place, overlooking a dimly lit garden. There were stairs somewhere that would allow her to descend into it, and she could see figures darting around, but she stayed where she was.

"What's Lord Pine's lovely human doing out here all alone?" a masculine voice asked, sliding up next to her and leaning back against the railing.

He was one of the men she'd danced with earlier. Lord Toro. He was about the same age as Pine, with devastatingly handsome dark hair he'd styled in Viking-like braids, who wore a black suit with accents of dark blue and a gemstone around his neck the size of a baby's fist.

He might have been hot, but she'd been glad the song they danced to was short. His hands had been threatening to roam, and he had a permanent leer that would take him from handsome to creepy if he wasn't careful.

"I have a name." It came out harsher than she intended, but at that point she didn't care.

"Lady Neve." He gave a slight bow of his head.

"Just Neve." If being a lady came with all this party bullshit, she wanted none of it.

"Just Neve, then." He reached out a hand but dropped it when he realized that Neve was holding her own arms close to her body.

Good. She'd been touched enough by strangers tonight.

"I couldn't help but overhearing your little ... discussion ... with Lord Pine. Parts of it, anyway. Are you alright?" He almost sounded sincere, but there was a serpentine quality to his voice.

Neve could recognize an opportunist when one slithered her way.

"Just tempers flaring from aching feet and a hot room," she lied. She wasn't sure why her first instinct was to defend Pine, but her instincts were screaming at her that Lord Toro was dangerous, and not in the sexy, fun way.

"Pine has always been delicate." He smirked the words out as if she was his co-conspirator.

Neve kept her mouth shut. Nothing about Pine had seemed delicate to her. The man was grieving and trying to keep his family together. He was doing the best he could, given the circumstances. Even so, she was still kind of pissed at him.

"A lady doesn't speak ill of her escort." Her parents had put her in etiquette lessons when she was ten, and it was disconcerting to hear Miss Emmeline's rules coming out of her own mouth. Of course, back then, Miss Emmeline had been admonishing her not to yell at Tommy, who kept trying to pluck a fancy clip from her hair.

The stakes felt a bit higher talking to Lord Toro.

"The music will be starting up again soon. Would you like to dance? Get whatever you're thinking off your mind?"

A lady also didn't turn down a dance from an appropriate suitor. But Miss Emmeline was in another galaxy, and she'd never know. "I'm sorry, I have to go."

Neve knew which dragon she'd rather take her chances with.

Pine wasn't far from where she'd left him. His face lit up for just a second as he saw her before he schooled his expression into something cool and casual.

Could there really be something there between them?

The smart move would be to demand a ride home right now and forget this whole thing. But when was Neve going to get an opportunity like this again?

"Two weeks," she said. "That's it. Then I'm gone."

Pine smiled. "You won't regret it."

8

Pine had to make things right with Neve.

Yes, she'd agreed to stay with him until the New Year's Ceremony despite everything. He didn't even care about the ceremony. Sometime during the night, it had occurred to him that she was about to go home, and he'd never see her again.

He couldn't have that.

Pine didn't want a mate. He didn't need a wife. But Neve was under his skin. She stoked the fire beating inside of him, and he couldn't let her go, not yet.

Two weeks. That was all he had, and he would have to make it count. If all went well, this thing between them would burn out, and he could send her off knowing exactly what it was like to have her.

And lose her.

No time to dwell on that.

Thinking about the last couple of days, Pine realized that he'd treated Neve more like a prisoner than an esteemed guest, and he was determined to change that now.

Briar had gone off to visit friends in the countryside, so now he and Neve were basically alone in the manor. It was the perfect setting to get this out of their systems. But Pine had never tried to seduce a woman like this before. He hadn't needed to. A bit of light flirtation, some dancing, and a few exchanged words to make sure they both knew the score had always been enough.

Not now. Not with this human.

It was all too delicate. She'd been ready to rip his head off when he agreed to the appearance at the New Year's Ceremony without consulting her. But Pine couldn't say he'd been thinking so much as panicking. Both in the face of the king's direct invitation and the realization that Neve was about to leave.

People left. People died. It was a fact of life.

But perhaps now was time to seize the moments he knew he had before they went away.

"You've got a serious look on your face," Neve observed as she entered the breakfast room. She took a seat and began selecting her food from the platters on the table. She was wearing tight fitting black pants and a crisscross striped, red top with buttons up the center. A hint of cleavage peaked out of the top, and Pine knew he was staring, but it took several beats for him to look away.

Those buttons were an invitation to sin. He wanted to pop them off one by one until the top hung open and bared her to him.

"Pine?" Neve prompted.

Right. Words. Not breasts.

"I thought we could go into the city today. There's a winter market that you might like. It's beautiful this time of year." And normally he ignored it to the best of his ability. It was filled with obnoxious children and bustling families who crowded all around him as if they'd never heard of the concept of personal space.

"I'd like to see that." She took a bite of a buttery roll and closed her eyes as bliss washed over her face, and she made a sound in the back of her throat that went straight to his cock.

"It will be cold," he said and tried to think of snow drifts and glaciers, of dips in icy lakes, anything to get his body under control.

"I brought a coat. You did lure me here under the guise of a winter getaway. I packed as appropriately as I could." She smiled as she said it, the anger from the night before gone.

"I am sorry about that." He'd apologize a hundred times if he had to. He never would have agreed to this if he knew the IDA would kidnap an innocent woman just to attend one party on the other side of the galaxy.

She waved him off and finished her breakfast.

An hour later they met in the entrance hall. Her tantalizing buttons were covered by a thick wool coat. A blue hat with a fuzzy ball on top covered her hair, and mittens with some sort of animal pattern enclosed her hands. It wasn't a style he'd seen on Vemion before, but there was something charming about all that wool.

He'd called for their transport earlier, and the vehicle was waiting outside for them. Pine assisted Neve into the vehicle and followed behind her.

Then they were off.

It was a short ride to the city, and Neve spent it pressed up against the window, watching as they drew closer and closer to civilization. His manor was within view of the castle, but with enough space between him and the city that it never felt too crowded. The royal city wasn't large. Some might have even called it a glorified village, but Pine liked it that way. He'd been to larger cities on Vemion, and they made his head spin.

Neve looked up and gasped. Pine leaned in next to her to see what she was looking at.

Two dragons in flight overhead, their paths weaving beside and around one another. Showing off. He'd seen it a hundred times, and it was nothing special. But Neve followed their every move with excitement, unable to suppress the sounds of joy and wonder that came out of her mouth.

He didn't watch the dragons. He watched her.

What had she done to him? How had she made it that he couldn't look away? Did they have sorcery on her planet? Some dark and enchanting magic that could hold a dragon in its spell?

It would be easy to blame this on witchcraft, but Pine didn't think it was anything so simple. Or complicated.

He wanted her. He'd wanted her from the moment she stepped off her ship.

He'd managed to pull away from that kiss, but

the effort had nearly brought him to his knees. If she kissed him again, there was no pulling back. Not now that he had two weeks with her.

The dragons disappeared behind some clouds, but by then they'd arrived outside the market, and the transport came to a stop.

The market was bordered by a fence made of tree branches except for red winter fruits that clung to a few twigs here and there. He knew from experience that eating the fruit would lead to a stomachache, and he would have warned Neve, but she didn't reach for it. Perhaps she had more restraint than he'd had as a boy.

Inside small stalls circled a square where a bonfire roared and families sat on benches or in small clusters, clutching cider and mulled wine as snow fell gently around them. A quartet in one corner played winter-themed tunes, old songs he remembered singing in the nursery with his nanny.

"So what's the winter story?" Neve asked. "What makes it so special?" She walked beside him as he made his way to a drinks vendor and ordered two ciders. Despite the temptation of the wine, Pine resisted. It was still a bit early for that.

"It's the winter festival," he said, handing her a steaming cider in a ceramic mug. "The harvest has died, ready to be born anew. Dragons gather together for warmth and safety. And we eat what food we've managed to save to spite the frost and dare nature not to provide us with a bounty next year."

"You *dare* nature not to bless your harvest?"

"Is that not how you do it?" He could hear why it might sound strange to someone unfamiliar with the practices on Vemion, but Pine had celebrated the winter rites every year, and they brought a solemn and defiant kind of comfort. "We're dragons; we don't beg anyone for anything."

"And what do you do to nature if she doesn't bless the harvest?" Neve asked.

"She?"

The human beside him gave him a look. "Everyone knows nature's a woman."

"Nature is far too complex to be any one gender. It's a force, not a person." Nature personified would be something terrible to behold.

For some reason, that made Neve laugh. She finished her cider and put her mug down on a small table full of dirty mugs before twining her arm with his. "Tell me more."

9

Neve was in a winter wonderland. And she wasn't even that cold.

Maybe it was the warmth from the cider. Maybe it was the bonfire.

She had a feeling it had something to do with the man, the dragon, beside her.

They'd left the winter festival behind some time ago and were now wandering the streets of the city, examining the window displays and dipping into any shop that caught their fancy.

Her fancy, actually.

She hadn't noticed it at first, but by the third shop, it was clear that Pine was following her lead. He hadn't suggested that they go into any store where she hadn't spent a good amount of time admiring their winter display, and once inside, he stuck close by, not caring about the wares for sale.

She hadn't planned to buy anything. She wasn't sure how dragon money worked, and she certainly didn't have any of her own. But Pine had put a stop to any of that thinking. In the first shop, he'd insisted that she get a scarf that shimmered in the light while still managing to ward off the cold. In the second shop, it was a small box of chocolates that tasted unlike anything she'd ever tried back home.

Now, in the third shop, she was trying her hardest not to look at the necklace on display.

A scarf and chocolates couldn't cost *that* much. Judging by the sparkle of the necklace, it had to cost a pretty penny. She wouldn't even try it on.

But her eyes kept dragging back to it.

Neve forced herself to walk away. And walking out of the store without a backwards glance was harder than it should have been.

"Shall we head home?" Pine asked when they reached the end of the main street without finding any more shops she couldn't resist.

Home.

For some reason, the thought of his manor sent a strange pang through her. This wasn't her home. It was a strange place, almost out of time, where she could experience impossible things with an impossible man and hope the memories stayed with her forever.

She shivered. It was getting chillier.

Pine called for their ride, and they waited on the sidewalk for it to pick them up. Then he cupped his hands together and blew into them.

Fire bloomed.

Dragon. Right. Definitely not what she was used to.

"Here," Pine said, "just be careful not to touch."

She let her hands hover over the flame, amazed that the heat was pleasant but never got too hot. A crazy part of her was convinced she could pull off her mitten and run her fingers through the flame like it was water and come out no worse for wear. Instead, she kept her hands safely out of range. Fire was fire, no matter what planet you were on.

The ride home—back to the manor—seemed shorter than the ride out. Once they were back inside, she and Pine stood in the entryway, neither of them seeming to know how to walk away.

All she had to do was lean forward to kiss him.

After this morning, she was almost sure he wouldn't run. But the memory of that first kiss a few days ago kept her rooted in place. Pine had rejected her once. One nice day couldn't wipe away the sting of that.

Finally, he took a step back. "We'll have supper in the informal dining room. I'm sure you'd like to rest after this morning."

They'd walked around town for a few hours; she hardly needed a nap. But, then again, she was on vacation.

They split up, and as Neve climbed the stairs to her room, her aching muscles told her that a nice long soak took priority over sleep. There was a gigantic tub in the bathroom in her suite, and it only took a few minutes to figure out how to work the faucet. She breathed out a sigh of relief when warm water started to flow. She didn't want to ask a servant to fill her bath—that seemed like a waste of their time.

She stripped off her clothes and climbed into the tub, letting out a moan of pure pleasure as she sank into the water. The tub was practically the size of a small swimming pool, and she could stretch out and let her whole body float if she wanted to.

Being a filthy rich dragon didn't suck.

Playing with the knobs and buttons on the side of the tub led to the discovery of how to turn on the tub's jets, and she also found the soap dispenser.

She stayed in the water until her hands were prunes and she feared she might actually dissolve into a liquid.

And once she was out of the tub, the nap was irresistible.

Ah, relaxation at its finest.

There was a dress waiting on a hanger outside her wardrobe later that day. She'd woken from her nap and wandered around the house like she was in some sort of country house mystery. Luckily, she didn't find any dead bodies or hear about any intrigue. Instead, she found a library full of books in a language she couldn't read. Apparently, her translator only worked on the spoken word.

Bummer.

But when she got back to her room, it was clear that it had been tidied and someone—Pine? —had selected a dress for her. It wasn't one that she'd brought. Instead, it was a light green flowing simple gown with shimmering golden details around the cuffs.

She wasn't sure how she felt about someone else choosing her clothes, but Neve couldn't resist touching the fabric.

Silk.

Or whatever the draconic equivalent to silk was. It felt decadent.

Would it really hurt to try it on?

No, absolutely not.

The dress fit like it was made for her, and when she twirled in front of her mirror, she couldn't stop the burst of laughter that came out of her mouth, not even when she clamped a hand over it.

She was keeping this dress when she went home.

Neve stopped spinning, and the smile slid off her face. Home. Right. She *wanted* to go home. She had a life back there. Theoretically. There was her job, which bored her out of her mind. And her family, who she avoided at all costs. Friends ... who she hadn't spent more than a couple of hours with since college.

Oh god, she didn't have a life.

Neve backed up until she basically collapsed onto her plush bed and shrank in on herself. Did anyone even realize she was gone? How long had she been gone for? She'd only been on Vemion a few days, but she had a vague idea that the universe was unfathomably big, and she remembered from old astronomy lessons that Earth was nowhere near any stars beside the sun. And she was pretty sure

Vemion wasn't in the solar system. Someone would have discovered it by now.

Could Pine actually send her home, or would it be some sort of Rip Van Winkle situation where she arrived after decades that had passed for her in a blink?

A chime sounded, the call to dinner.

Neve pushed those thoughts aside. It had been a very nice day. She was wearing a beautiful dress. And she'd agreed to hang around for two weeks. She'd worry about the future tomorrow.

The worries fell away with each step towards the informal dining room, where Pine was waiting for her. She'd be lying if she said her heart didn't start to race a bit.

She'd thought he would kiss her earlier. She'd hoped he would.

If he kissed her tonight, she wasn't holding back.

The informal dining room was still nicer than anything that Neve had seen outside of Vemion. The table could fit about six people and was held up by gilt legs and had a small candelabra in the center.

Pine was already seated and stood when she entered. "The dress ..." He trailed off, eyes raking over her.

She could feel her cheeks turning red and willed

her blush to fade. "It's not too bad. It even has pock-ets." She stuck her hands as deep as they could go to show them off.

They might have stood there staring at each other like fools if a servant hadn't entered bearing two plates. Neve took her seat. So did Pine.

She barely tasted the food.

The whole meal, she couldn't stop looking at him. The way he held his fork-like utensil. The delicate way he patted at his mouth after eating a particularly saucy morsel. They way he'd look up every so often, and the candlelight would reflect in his eyes, making it look like they were lit with an inner fire.

When the last of the plates were cleared away, Pine held out a hand. "Walk with me?"

Like she could say no to that.

Neve placed her hand in his and had to suppress the shiver that tried to travel from her fingers down her spine and through the rest of her body. They were barely touching. No need to make such a big deal out of it.

Pine led her towards a glass door that led outside. If anything could break the enchantment between them, it was the chill of winter. Her dress was beautiful, but it wouldn't keep her warm outside.

It wasn't an issue.

The door led to a glass enclosed atrium that sparkled with a mix of candlelight and subtle electric light. It looked like something out of a fairy tale. And it was warm. She could feel the heat even through her dress.

She could feel Pine's hand in hers and his breath on her neck.

"What is this ..." She wasn't sure.

"The winter garden," Pine filled in. "It's protected from the cold and can grow plants that would freeze or die outside."

Neve didn't care about the plants. She cared about the way Pine was looking at her, the way his thumb was rubbing against the back of her hand.

She didn't wait for him to make the first move. She turned towards him and lifted her chin.

"Kiss me."

His lips were on hers a second later. It was different than their first kiss. Confident. Gentle. Reverent.

Pine wasn't running away.

He had her pressed against the glass, the light from the atrium giving him a hazy halo.

"Beautiful," he whispered.

Neve didn't think he was talking about the flowers.

She couldn't stand it. She grabbed the lapels of his suit and pulled him down for another kiss. Her lips parted, and their tongues collided. Pine groaned, and his hand was suddenly in her hair, tangling and tugging just enough to make her shiver.

She felt his other hand slide down her side and cup her ass.

Oh, yes.

"We shouldn't be doing this," he whispered in her ear.

"Why not?" She arched her back, pressing herself against him.

"Because ..." He trailed off, letting kisses rain down her throat. "Because I have a whole suite upstairs and a very comfortable bed. Join me?"

10

Neve lay naked on Pine's bed, her body clenched in anticipation and raw desire. She watched, breathless, as the dragon man shed the last of his clothes, each movement deliberate and tantalizingly slow. Her body burned with a need that bordered on pain. If he didn't touch her again soon, she might actually combust.

Instead, Pine stood there, his eyes roaming over her with an intensity that sent shivers down her spine. No candles flickered this time, but she saw the fire in his gaze, a fiery passion that mirrored her own. Dragon, she remembered, the realization adding a thrilling edge of danger to her hunger.

Her dragon.

For now.

If he intended to look at her all night, she might as well return the favor. As if it were a hardship to stare at the most gorgeous man she'd ever seen. His chest was broad, muscles sculpted and defined, inviting her touch. His hips tapered in a way that made her long to lick and kiss every inch of his skin. The sight of him, all raw masculinity and primal power, was almost too much to bear.

Pine's cock was hard and thick, curving towards his belly in a way that made her mouth water and her core throb with want. She wanted him inside her, filling her completely. The rest of him was equally magnificent, every part of his body honed to perfection. Her wildest fantasies would need to work overtime to dream him up.

Her hands ached to touch him, to feel the heat of his skin against hers. But Pine remained still, his gaze locked onto her, drinking her in like she was a feast laid out just for him. The anticipation was killing her, yet the wait built a tension that promised an explosive release. She held on, reveling in this moment of pure, unadulterated desire.

"I'm naked and in your bed," she whispered, her voice hoarse with desire. "Are you waiting for an engraved invitation?" The words came out sharper than she intended, but if he didn't touch her soon, she would go crazy.

A slow, predatory smile spread across Pine's face as he moved towards her, his hips swaying in a way that made her heart pound. He leaned over the bed, his hands planted on either side of her, caging her in. His breath tickled her face, hot and sweet, as he whispered, "I just wanted to look at you. To memorize everything. You're a fucking masterpiece, Neve."

His words sent a shiver of pleasure down her spine. She reached up, grabbing his shoulders and pulling him down on top of her. The kiss was passionate, messy. Perfect. His tongue parted her lips, sweeping into her mouth, exploring her with a hunger that matched her own. Her breasts pressed against his chest, her nipples hardening from the delicious friction.

Pine groaned into her mouth, a sound that reverberated through her, stoking the fire within. He shifted until he was half on top of her, his thigh pressing against her core, making her gasp.

She needed him inside her, to fill the aching void that only he could satisfy. Every touch, every kiss, every whispered word was a promise of the ecstasy to come. Her body hummed with anticipation, and she knew that this night would be one she'd never forget.

But he was taking his time, kissing her like she was a work of art, his hands exploring her body like he was trying to map it. She felt his fingers trail down her belly and over the sensitive skin of her thighs.

"Pine," she whispered, a plea.

"No need to rush," he replied, his fingers sliding farther until they dipped between her legs.

Neve bucked against him, unable to contain her reaction. He was a fucking tease, and she was so ready for him.

"Please," she moaned as his fingers delved deeper, exploring her slick folds.

"I'm going to devour you," he breathed against her ear, a dark promise.

And then he was sliding down her body until his head was right there between her legs. She barely had a chance to think or react before his tongue was on her, licking and sucking like she was his dessert, not the sweet concoction they'd had at dinner. His tongue found her core and teased her, making her grab a pillow to smother her moans. She couldn't control the sounds escaping her lips. She was close, so close.

Neve's climax hit her like a tidal wave, her body arching off the bed as a burst of fire ignited within her. Her eyes fluttered closed, the sensation overwhelming her senses. She was barely aware of Pine sliding back up her body, his skin hot and slick with sweat. She felt the weight of him settling over her, his breath ragged and urgent against her neck. He positioned himself at her entrance, the anticipation making her tremble.

He slid inside her slowly, inch by inch, every movement deliberate and controlled. His eyes locked on hers, the intensity in his gaze making her heart race. She could see the raw desire and something deeper, something more profound, reflected in those piercing eyes. She felt every inch of him filling her, stretching her, and she couldn't look away. It was like they were connected in a way that transcended the physical, their souls intertwining.

"You're perfect," he whispered, his voice a low growl that sent shivers down her spine. The words were a caress, tender and filled with a reverence that made her chest ache. She was too far gone to respond, too consumed by the feelings coursing through her body.

Pine began to thrust, each movement deliberate and powerful. She gasped with every stroke, her nails digging into his shoulders. He was a solid wall above her, driving into her like he was claiming her, like he couldn't get enough. The room filled with the sound of their bodies coming together, the rhythm intense and primal.

"Harder," she demanded, her voice husky and needy. She wanted to feel him completely, to be consumed by him.

He obliged, his hips pumping faster, the force of his thrusts pushing her farther into the mattress. She could feel his heartbeat hammering against her chest, echoing her own frantic rhythm. The connection between them was electric, a spark that ignited every nerve in her body. She was lost in him, in the moment, in the raw intensity of their connection. It was more than just physical; it was a fusion of souls, a dance of desire and need.

Neve could feel the heat building inside her again, her body coiling tighter as Pine moved above her. His eyes were locked onto hers, the fire in them burning hotter than ever. She could barely hold his gaze, the intensity of his stare making her feel both vulnerable and powerful. His breaths were ragged, matching her own, and she could feel his heart pounding against her chest, their bodies syncing in a rhythm that felt uniquely theirs.

"Come for me, Neve." His voice was raw, a ragged whisper that sent shivers down her spine. It was more than a request; it was a plea, a need that echoed her own. She didn't want to deny him. She couldn't. Her body was already too far gone, spiraling towards the edge.

The second wave hit her hard, crashing over her like a storm. She let out a sound that was half moan, half scream, her body arching off the bed as every nerve ending sparked with pleasure. Her hands clutched at him, nails digging into his shoulders as if he were the only thing anchoring her to the world.

Pine followed her a few seconds later, his body stiffening as he spilled inside her. His groan was low and deep, resonating through her. She could feel his release, his heat filling her, and it sent another shudder through her body. His heartbeat hammered against her chest, a wild drumbeat that matched her own racing pulse.

They stayed like that for a few minutes, neither of them seeming to be able to move. His body was heavy on hers, a comforting weight that made her feel safe and protected. She could feel the rise and fall of his chest, the slowing of his heartbeat as they both came down from their high. Their skin was slick with sweat, their breaths mingling in the small space between their lips.

Neve couldn't find the words to express it, but this might have been the most intimate thing she'd ever experienced. She felt connected to Pine in a way she never had with anyone else. It was more than just physical; it was emotional, raw, and real.

And she still had two whole weeks with this dragon man beside her.

11

Nine days later, Neve was bundled up tight and jogging to keep up with Pine as they walked to the edge of his territory. The snow crunched beneath their boots, and a chill wind whipped through her layers, but the excitement bubbling inside her kept her warm.

Pine had promised to take her flying today, and this time she was determined to enjoy it. That first day on Vemion seemed so long ago now, and she'd been so convinced that she was crazy that she hadn't taken any time to truly enjoy what was going on.

The approached a small clearing. Today, Pine seemed to be staying clear of the cliffs. It was chillier and windier and no doubt more dangerous to fly.

Neve didn't care. She wanted to soar.

The last nine days had been like something out of a dream. One night in Pine's bed had lead to another, and by the third, there was no question about where she was sleeping. Now the only real question was whether they would get out of bed at all.

Then today, he'd asked if she wanted to fly, and Neve couldn't say no.

"This should do," Pine said. "Are you ready?"

"Hell yeah." She would have been smiling wider, but her cheeks were stuck in a grimace against the biting wind. Pine had rustled up a thicker jacket and more appropriate winter wear, but it could only do so much when the temperatures had dropped to something even polar bears might find a bit chilly.

He gave her a happy smile and closed his eyes, breathing deep. For a moment, the air shimmered around him, and then there was a dragon, all shimmering blue scales and claws standing before her.

When the transformation was complete, he lowered his head, inviting her to climb aboard. Neve complied, hauling herself up and settling between his massive shoulder blades. She gripped the ridges of his scales, heart racing with anticipation.

With a powerful thrust of his wings, Pine

launched them up into the air. She let out a surprised shriek as they soared higher and higher, the ground falling away beneath them. If she looked down, her stomach roiled, and she wondered just how safe this could be.

Did they make seat belts for dragon riders?

The wind whipped through her hair and stung her eyes, but she refused to look away, drinking in the breathtaking view that unfolded before them.

From up here, Neve could see for miles—the distant glittering stone in the capital city, the frozen lakes and rivers snaking across the landscape, the endless sweep of snow-capped mountains.

Neve had never experienced anything like this before. It was exhilarating and terrifying all at once, setting her heart racing. Was this what skydiving or bungee jumping felt like?

She risked a glance downwards, her stomach lurching as she registered just how far the ground was. Squeezing her eyes shut for a moment, Neve focused on the warmth of Pine's scales beneath her hands, the steady rhythm of his wings.

Slowly, Neve's worries began to subside, and the joy of the ride swept her up in its embrace.

Let's see how you like this.

She could have sworn she heard Pine's words in

her head, but that was impossible. It wasn't like he could have vocal cords as a dragon, could he? Were dragons telepathic?

Before she could question it out loud, Pine banked sharply, and Neve gasped as they began to descend, spiraling down towards the snow-covered landscape. Just when she was certain they were going to crash, Pine leveled out, skimming just above the treetops before climbing once more.

Neve's breath caught in her throat, her pulse pounding. This was more than a flight; it felt like a dance, an intricate waltz swayed out against the backdrop of the winter sky.

"Faster!" she shouted, urging him on with eager laughter, her voice swallowed by the howling wind.

Pine responded with a sudden surge, his wings beating with powerful strokes, and they shot upwards like an arrow released from a bow.

Neve flattened herself against his back, sure she was about to fall off but too excited to care. She let out another laugh, a bubbling sound of pure joy, echoing through the vast expanse as they climbed higher still. Beneath them, the world became an abstract landscape of whites and blues, indistinct and distant.

It should have been colder, but Pine was a

furnace beneath her, his scales emanating heat from the fire that must live inside of him.

She never wanted this to end.

Adrenaline kept her giddy, but there were more feelings jumbled up inside of her, fear and melancholy and worry. Not that she would fall. Even if it was crazy to believe, she knew that Pine would catch her.

No, she was worried about what would happen in a few days once they were done with the New Year's Celebration.

She was supposed to go home. That was the deal, the one that she'd insisted on. And now she clung even tighter to Pine's scales and tried not to think about what that would mean.

Each moment spent with Pine felt like a gift, but unlike a gift, their time was limited. How would she ever be able to go home after this?

She clung to Pine and pushed the thought aside.

The world faded beneath her again as they began to dive, the rush of air whipping around them in a wild frenzy. Pine twisted in mid-air, his powerful wings cutting through the wind as he performed a maneuver that sent a thrill down Neve's spine. She screamed, half in joy and half in fright, and found herself laughing uncontrollably as they soared upwards once more, the ground spiraling far below.

Pine evened out and they glided on the wind for several moments until she saw the ground getting closer and realized they were descending.

Pine landed, and Neve slid off of him on wobbly legs. They were at the edge of the woods, and the trees did something to block the wind, but it was still bitterly cold, and she regretted not having the dragon under her to keep her warm.

"Come see this." Pine held out a hand.

Neve took it. He led her deeper into the forest, where the trees towered over them high enough to block out a lot of the sun, their branches heavy with glimmering icicles sparkling like diamonds. The stark beauty encased in snow felt enchanted, like a realm that existed out of time and place.

That's what these weeks with Pine were—something unreal. No matter what she wanted.

"Here," he said, stopping in a small clearing where light poured through the branches above, illuminating a steaming pond. "Are you ready for a swim?"

Neve stared at Pine in disbelief. "Are you serious? It's freezing." He had to be joking. But the steam coming off the pond did feel nice.

His eyes sparkled with mischief, and he grinned. "Are you scared?"

She knew she was being played even as she slipped out of her coat and tossed her gloves aside. "Not a chance, buddy."

Pine laughed and began to remove his outer layers, glancing over to ensure she was still with him. She wasn't sure why dragons kept their clothes on when they changed shape. Every movie with werewolves she'd ever seen ended with tattered piles of fabric when they shifted. But that was fiction. This was real life.

She reached for the buttons of her shirt, fingers trembling from the cold and from growing anticipation. The moment she shed her layers, the frigid air tried to tear her to pieces. But the beauty of the forest around her—and the man in front of her—kept her going.

She didn't waste time admiring anything else as she slipped out of the last of her clothes and sprinted for the spring.

Neve plunged into the steaming water, gasping as the heat enveloped her, in stark contrast to the biting cold of the air. The sensation was immediate and intoxicating, washing over her and loosening the tension still coiled tightly in her muscles. Riding a dragon was an incredible experience, but it was hell on her quads.

She surfaced, laughter bubbling up as she turned to Pine, who had just stepped into the pond. The steam danced around him, wrapping him in a misty veil that highlighted the strong lines of his body.

Pine flashed a wicked smile, eyes gleaming. "Hot enough for you?"

Neve splashed water at him. "It's getting there."

Pine's deep rumble of a laugh echoed through the forest as he waded deeper into the water. He took his time, as if the cold air didn't bother him one bit. She watched as the steaming water lapped against his chest, highlighting every sculpted muscle, every line of strength. His eyes met hers, holding a world of unspoken promises.

It would hurt so badly when she left, she could feel it in her bones.

She refused to dwell.

Neve felt a blush creep up her cheeks, the heat of the spring doing little to disguise her body's reaction to Pine's presence. She couldn't look away from him.

Pine moved closer, his hands reaching out to gently brush her arms. Despite the warmth of the water, his touch sent shivers down her spine. He leaned in, his breath a whisper against her ear. "What are you thinking about?"

She leaned into the embrace. "This is ..." She trailed off, unsure of what to say.

He cupped her face in his hands, gaze intense. "Yes. It is."

He kissed her and Neve melted into it, the warmth of Pine's lips a stark contrast to the crisp air that still pricked at her cheeks. The steam from the hot spring wrapped around them like a cocoon, isolating them from the world and giving them a moment that was solely theirs.

She could taste the faintest hint of smoke on his tongue, a reminder of the dragon that lurked beneath his masculine exterior.

And what a masculine exterior it was.

Pine's hands slid from her face, tracing a path down her neck and along her shoulders before settling on her hips under the water. He pulled her closer, their bodies pressing together as the kiss deepened. Neve could feel his heart pounding against her chest, echoing the rhythm of her own. Despite the heat of the spring, she shivered.

When they finally broke apart, Pine rested his

forehead against hers, his breath coming in ragged gasps. "You have no idea what you do to me."

Neve's heart nearly broke at the vulnerability she heard. "I want you," she replied softly, her thumbs tracing the line of his jaw.

Pine closed his eyes, leaning into her touch. When he opened them again, there was a fire in his gaze that sent a thrill down Neve's spine. "Mine," he growled, his voice low and primal.

Her breath hitched in her throat, the intensity of the word like an embrace. She tried to speak, but all that came out was a soft whimper, a sound of surrender and desire.

Pine's grip on her tightened, a possessive claim that raised goosebumps across her skin, despite the heat of the water. His lips trailed along her jawline, each kiss a brand searing into her soul. Neve's fingers threaded through his damp hair, pulling him closer, as if afraid he might vanish like a wisp of smoke.

The world around them faded into a blur of sensation and emotion. Here, in this secluded haven, they were the only two beings that mattered.

Pine's hands caressed her body, mapping out her curves with a reverence that made her feel worshipped. Neve arched into his touch, feeling the contours of his chest against her own questing fingers, the defined muscles of his arms. Strength was written across every muscle, every dimple, a promise of what he would do to those who crossed him and a vow to protect those he held close.

The water lapped at their skin, the heat and cold only heightening the intensity. Pine's lips found hers again, and the kiss was a fusion of hunger and desperate care.

When he found her entrance, she groaned, wrapping her legs tight around his waist as they moved together.

Pine was deliberate, his face a mask of seductive concentration as he drove into her, gaze never leaving hers. It was intense, almost too much, but she clung to him hard enough to bruise.

The tension coiled tighter and tighter, making little noises escape her mouth as Pine hit her just right until she couldn't hold it back any longer, breaking apart against him as she came. With a roar, he emptied himself inside of her, whispering her name into her neck as he held her close.

It was almost too hot in the spring now, but Neve never wanted to leave this secret oasis, and from the way Pine was holding her, she was almost certain he felt the same.

12

Neve didn't want to go. She snuggled closer into the warmth of Pine's body and tried not to think about what the rest of the day would bring.

The New Year's Celebration.

The end of ... this.

Two weeks ago, she'd be running for the spaceship. Two weeks ago, she'd be happy to put this all behind her as a weird and impossible memory.

Two weeks ago, she hadn't fallen in love.

She squeezed her eyes shut and tried to keep her groan to herself.

The sun poured through the window, illuminating the room in a dreamy soft glow. Pine was a soothing presence beside her; his deep, rhythmic breaths were calming the storm of doubts swirling in her mind. She wanted to freeze this moment and make it last forever, but she couldn't ignore the fact that this was their last day together, and soon she'd have to go home.

She woke Pine with kisses, and they stayed in bed until the sun was high in the sky, but eventually they had to get up.

"I think you'll like the dress," Pine told her as he reluctantly let go of her hand so she could head to her room to get ready.

After the silver dress he'd given her, Neve had trusted him to order her a dress for the New Year's Ceremony. "I'm sure I'll love it."

The moment hung between them, the words loaded with much more, but Neve couldn't bring herself to confess. It was too much, too vulnerable.

What if he didn't feel the same?

She fled to her room and had to stifle a gasp when she saw the dress waiting for her.

It was a breathtaking creation, a deep sapphire blue that shimmered with an inner light. The fabric flowed like water, cascading down to the floor in elegant folds.

Delicate silver embroidery adorned the bodice,

intricate patterns swirling across the fabric that reminded her of frost on a windowpane. The neckline dipped low, accentuated by off-the-shoulder sleeves that would leave her collarbone exposed.

As she ran her fingers over the material, Neve felt a lump form in her throat. This wasn't just a dress; it was a statement. Pine had chosen something that would make her stand out. A man didn't give a woman a dress like this if he didn't feel something.

With trembling hands, she slipped into the gown. It fit like a glove, as if it had been crafted specifically for her body. When she looked in the mirror, she barely recognized herself. The woman staring back at her looked regal, powerful, and undeniably loved.

For a moment, Neve allowed herself to imagine a future where she belonged in this world, where she could stand beside Pine as his. What would it be like to be loved like that? To never doubt it? To not put conditions on it?

She had to push the thoughts aside.

Hair and makeup were not something she could do on her own, but the same maid who had helped her get ready for the Yule Ball what felt like a million years ago helped her again.

The maid did an admirable job and then left, leaving Neve to contemplate her fate.

Ugh. She was being dramatic. It was a party, not a firing squad.

The door cracked open, and Pine stuck his head in. "May I join you?"

Neve smoothed her hands over the bodice of her dress. "Of course."

He entered the room, and Neve's heart stuttered. He was resplendent in formal attire that perfectly complemented her gown. No one would question that they belonged together.

He wore a tailored jacket of deep midnight blue, almost black, with intricate silver embroidery along the lapels and cuffs that mirrored the patterns on her dress. The jacket fit him perfectly, accentuating his broad shoulders and trim waist. Underneath, he wore a crisp white shirt with a high collar, fastened with a silver pin that gleamed in the light. His trousers were the same deep blue as the jacket, falling in a clean line to polished black boots.

His hair was styled neatly, emphasizing the sharp angles of his face. As he moved closer, Neve caught a whiff of a spicy, smoky scent that was uniquely Pine.

He looked …

Damn it, they didn't have enough time for her to rip his clothes off and show him exactly what that outfit was doing for her.

He had a black box in his hands that was about the size of a folder and an inch or two thick. A jewelry box.

"I thought this would complete the look." Pine opened the box and showed her a gorgeous sapphire necklace set in silver and diamonds. The sapphires gleamed, their deep blue hue a perfect match for her dress. The intricate silver setting and twinkling diamonds added a level of elegance that took her breath away.

"Pine, it's … gorgeous," she whispered, her fingers hovering over the jewels but not quite touching them. The necklace had to be far too expensive … or priceless. It was meant for a princess, not some normal girl from Earth.

He stepped closer, his eyes intense as they locked with hers. "Will you wear it?"

Her heart raced as she nodded, words caught in her throat. Pine carefully lifted the necklace from its velvet cushion and moved behind her. Neve swept her hair to the side, exposing her neck. She shivered as his fingers brushed against her skin, gently fastening the clasp.

The weight of the necklace settled against her collarbone, cool at first but quickly warming to her skin. When Pine's hands came to rest on her shoulders, she leaned back into his touch, savoring the moment.

"Look," he murmured, guiding her to face the mirror.

The necklace was the perfect finishing touch. It nestled perfectly in the dip of her neckline, drawing attention to the elegant curve of her neck and the bare expanse of her shoulders.

"Beautiful," Pine said, his eyes meeting hers in the mirror. The pride and affection in his gaze made her heart ache.

He wasn't talking about the necklace.

Neve turned to face him, her hands coming to rest on his chest. She couldn't just leave without telling him how she felt. "I ," she began, struggling to find the right words.

Before she could gather up the rest of her courage, a servant knocked on the door to let them know the carriage was waiting. Neve hated how relieved she felt.

She laced her arm through Pine's, and they

headed for the celebration.

Pine didn't tell Neve she was wearing his mother's necklace. When he'd spoken with the dressmaker, he had the necklace in mind, but he hadn't been sure that he would put it on her neck.

Now he couldn't stop staring. The necklace glimmered against her skin, catching the light with every movement. It was as if it had been made for her, though he knew its history stretched back generations in his family.

Perhaps not made for her, but *meant* for her.

His mother's necklace. An heirloom passed down through the centuries, worn by the most revered dragon ladies of his lineage. And now it graced Neve's neck, looking more at home there than he could have ever imagined.

He hadn't told her its significance. Part of him was afraid—afraid of what it might mean, afraid of her reaction. The past two weeks had been paradise, but they hadn't spoken of anything that might come beyond them, and Pine hadn't asked her to stay on Vemion.

How could he? She belonged back on Earth. She

had a family there, a life there. What could he offer her besides jewels and his heart?

The New Year's Ceremony was a fete much like the Yule Ball. Dragon lords and ladies from across the kingdom came and showed off in their finery. They danced for the king and dazzled each other with their wit and wealth.

Pine would have gone mad without Neve by his side.

And when the orchestra began to play, it was only natural that he held out his hand and invited his woman to the dance floor.

As the music began, Pine placed his hand on Neve's waist, drawing her close. There was a proper distance he was supposed to maintain, a nod towards propriety, but he didn't give a damn.

"They're staring at us," Neve whispered as he pulled her close before a spin.

"They're admiring you," he murmured back.

A blush crept up Neve's cheeks. Pine's heart felt stuck in a vise. How could he let her go? How could he watch her walk away, knowing that he would never see her again?

They danced through the song and into another, and Pine started to feel even more eyes on them. These weren't in envy.

Something was going on.

"Pine," Neve said softly, her voice barely audible above the music. "There's something I want to say."

He'd dealt with nerves before. He was a dragon lord, a man who could stand before an army and hold it off until help arrived. At least in theory, he'd never needed to prove that to anyone. But it felt like Neve held his life in her hands.

One word, and he would shatter.

Her tongue darted out to lick her lips, and she took a deep breath. "I—"

There was a crash behind them, followed by the loud marching steps of soldiers. "Lord Pine!" A voice boomed as the entire party ground to a halt around them. "By order of the king, you are under arrest for treason!"

The guards swept in, pushing Neve out of the way before surrounding Pine, pikes and fireproof shields held in their hand. The head guardsman held dragon fire in his palm, a threat and a promise of what would happen if Pine resisted.

"What are you doing? Stop!" Neve struggled against one of the guards, trying to get to him.

Their eyes met, and his heart leapt at the emotion he saw on her face. But he didn't dare to hope it was real. Not for him.

"It will be alright," he told her, ignoring the guards but staying still. "Find Briar. I'm sure this is some misunderstanding."

Before he could say anything else, the guards rushed him away.

13

Neve stood in shock as the guards surrounded Pine and shouldered her out of the way. Her heart hammered in her chest, disbelief coursing through her veins as even more guards poured into the ballroom.

The room buzzed with eager anticipation, whispers like a swarm of biting insects, but all she could focus on was the torment etched on Pine's face.

"Stop!" she shouted, her voice breaking through the chaos. The guards ignored her as they began to usher Pine away in an impenetrable wall of pikes and men.

A desperate adrenaline spurred her forward to try and free Pine, but a guard loomed before her, blocking her path. She pushed past him, heart racing. What was going on? How could this happen?

The dragged Pine away, leaving her alone in the ballroom surrounded by dragons eager to see how this would play out. Neve wanted to scream at them, to demand they do something about the injustice going on. But the expectation in the air hung thick. These lords and ladies wanted her to make a scene; they wanted the entertainment.

Who cared about a man's freedom when there was entertainment to be had?

She needed to figure out what was going on and find out how to help Pine. She had to protect him. Instinct drove her out of the ballroom and into the hallway, away from the grinning courtiers. If anyone could help her, it was Briar. She had to find Pine's sister so they could do whatever came next.

Did dragons have lawyers?

In the hallway, the echoes of laughter and music faded into eerie silence. Without any other idea, she walked on, expecting to be stopped at any moment. If they were really worried about treason, shouldn't the place be crawling with security? Neve furtively glanced down the corridor and quickened her pace, her pulse quickening as she heard whispers drifting from another room. She pressed her back against the cool stone wall, straining to catch snippets of conversation.

"... heard he wants to overthrow the king ..."

"... Lord Toro said that scum's been planning this for years ..."

"I heard he said something to that human amusement of his. Wouldn't be surprised if he did his father in. I never trusted him."

Anger heated her blood, and Neve could have sworn she felt her fingertips get red with actual fire. If she had Pine's powers right now, she'd burn this place to the ground.

She scrambled to remember what she and Pine had even argued about. It all seemed so long ago now. She'd wanted to go home; he asked her to say. Had they even said something about the king? Neve couldn't remember. They certainly hadn't talked about treason.

She had to find Briar.

A part of her wanted to hunt down Lord Toro and give him a piece of her mind. She hadn't thought of him at all in the past two weeks, but she'd known there was something off about the way he was talking to her. She'd thought he was just a creep, not that he was scheming to get her ... Pine in trouble.

She kept moving, slipping into the shadows as she heard more whispering voices. Peering around the corner, she spotted a servant carrying a stack of papers, clearly anxious and whispering hurriedly to a group of guards huddled together.

"Lord Toro said these must be signed by the prisoner. He demands his confession," the servant said, a quiver of fear in his voice.

Neve gritted her teeth as she listened to the servant. She couldn't believe what she was hearing. Lord Toro was orchestrating this entire charade, and he expected Pine to play along. Did he really think no one would stop him?

She was going to. She knew the truth.

Frankly, she wouldn't care if Pine *had* been conspiring against the king. She didn't care about kings or princes or whoever was in charge; she just cared for her dragon lord.

More than cared for, if she was being honest.

She had the shape of the plot in her head now. Lord Toro had accused Pine of treason. For some reason, the king had believed him. And if she didn't find Pine soon, they'd make him sign a false confession, and then ...

Well, she wasn't sure what they did to traitors here, but it couldn't be anything good.

Was Pine being kept in some dungeon somewhere? Would they torture him? She wanted to find him and set him free, but she had no idea where to look or if he was even in the palace. For all she knew, there was a prison on the other side of town where he'd be locked away in a tower forever.

She had to act now.

Neve crept closer to the group, her mind racing. She needed information, and she needed it fast. The servant clearly knew something, and the guards had walked away. If she was going to take a risk, she needed to take it now.

She took a deep breath and stepped out of the shadows, approaching the servant confidently. "Excuse me, I couldn't help but overhear your conversation. What's happening to Lord Pine? There was some sort of commotion in the ballroom, but I missed it all."

The servant jumped, clutching papers to his chest. "M-Miss, you shouldn't be out here." His eyes darted around nervously.

"Please." She tried not to sound desperate, but it was getting hard not to. "Where did they take him?" All thoughts of pretending she was some uninterested third party had evaporated. She wasn't good at playing a part. She just wanted Pine back.

The servant's eyes widened as the beat of boots on the ground announced the guards returning, and he quickly turned to address them. "The human was asking about Lord Pine."

Damn it!

"That's not true!" Maybe throwing a fit would throw them off, but one grabbed her by the arm hard enough to bruise before she could even try.

"His lordship said to be on the lookout for the pet human," said the guard holding her.

"Take her into custody," said the other one. "Lord Toro will want to question her himself."

Neve's stomach twisted with dread as the guard's hands closed even more firmly around her arms. She looked frantically down the corridor, hoping against hope that Briar or someone else might come to her aid, but the hallway remained frustratingly empty.

As the guards marched her away, Neve's mind raced, desperately searching for a way to escape and find Pine. She couldn't give up, not when he needed her. But the iron grip of the guard left her with little room to maneuver, and the fear of what might happen to Pine if she resisted only fueled her growing sense of helplessness.

She couldn't help him from inside a cage. But she had no idea how she was going to get out of this mess.

14

The manacles around Pine's wrists rubbed his skin raw. His teeth chattered against the cold, and when he'd tried to summon flame to warm himself up, nothing had happened.

There was something in the metal that interfered with his powers.

He'd heard of such a thing but had never expected to experience it for himself. He still wasn't sure what was going on or how he'd ended up in this situation. He wasn't in a cell, not technically. If he had to guess, someone had stripped guest quarters bare so there was nothing he could work with except for a chair, and then he'd been locked in. He was still a lord, after all; they didn't throw lords in the dungeons.

Not immediately.

Was Neve alright? What would happen to her if he was executed for a treason he hadn't committed?

The door opened, and Pine surged to his feet as if he might be able to rush the guards and escape. Instead, Lord Toro walked in. The man was a few years older than him, and they'd never gotten along. There'd always been something ... off about Toro. He'd been a schemer and a social climber, and Pine wanted nothing to do with it.

"I always knew you'd end up in cage." Toro smirked at him as he leaned against the wall. He summoned a ball of flame and tossed it from hand to hand. "Never thought I'd be the one to put you there."

"What are you doing? Why?" Pine watched the fire dance back and forth and tried not to think about how he was cut off from his own.

"I'm framing you for treason and stealing your lands." Toro's smirk turned into a broad smile. "You made it easy for me. Inviting that human to stay and flaunting her around, not paying attention to anything else. It's an awfully disruptive time when a lord ascends to his title, and you haven't done a thing to secure your position."

Pine's heart sank, and his stomach churned.

Neve had become a pawn in Toro's twisted game. The memory of her laughter and warmth clashed violently with the coldness surrounding him now. "She has nothing to do with this," he growled, struggling against the chains that bound him.

Toro laughed, a mocking sound that echoed in the empty room. "Of course she does. It's her words that sealed your fate." He edged closer, eyes glinting with malice. "And I intend to use her against you, every way I can."

"Touch her," Pine said, his voice low and dangerous, "and die."

Toro's eyes flicked up and down, taking him in. "You know, I might actually believe you. A shame, really. You could have been useful. I—"

Someone banged on the door, and Toro gritted his teeth. "What?" he demanded.

Two guards came in, dragging a bedraggled Neve behind them. "We found this one wandering the halls. You said to be on the lookout, my lord."

"I didn't say to bring her *here*." He scowled. "You may as well leave her with him. Find the sister; we need to take care of her."

They shoved Neve inside, and Toro left with the guards. Neve fell to the floor, and Pine surged forward to grab her, but the manacles made it impossible to do much to help.

She pushed herself up from off the ground, eyes wild. "Are you alright?"

He nodded. "It will be alright, I promise," he lied. "Did you find Briar? What's going on out there?" He wanted to punch Toro—or do something worse—but that wasn't an option right now. He had to get Neve out of this mess, then he could worry about himself.

"They caught me before I could," she said. "How can they think you're a traitor?"

"Toro came to gloat. By the laws of Vemion, he'll have rights to my lands if I'm found guilty. I don't understand how he can do this. There's no evidence." Pine curled his hands into fists.

"He wants you to sign a confession." Neve stood like a queen, her shoulders pulled back and chin held high. The sapphire necklace still hung on her neck, the unspoken declaration of his affection. Her dress was a bit rumpled, but not torn.

Some pair they made.

"I'm not signing anything." Pine stood. His hand might have been bound, but at least he wasn't chained to the wall. "Please, sit. We may be here for awhile."

Neve spun around and approached the door, testing the handle and finding it locked. "We can't just wait around for Toro to hatch his plan. We have to ..." She faltered. "I'm really not sure what we have to do. Talk to a lawyer? The king? Is there anyone who can intercede for us?"

Us.

Despite the hopelessness of the situation, Pine almost smiled. Neve could have walked away. Instead, she'd chosen to stay with him, to fight with him.

He wouldn't let her die with him.

"Can you breathe fire or something and get us out of here? This door is made of wood." She ran her fingers over it, and if she'd had claws, they would have left gouges. She was clearly ready to fight.

Pine held up his manacled hands. "There's something in the metal that blocks my abilities. I can't summon my fire or shift." Not that shifting would have done him much good. He would destroy the room and crush Neve in the process, and the window was far too small for him to fit through as a man, let alone a dragon.

Neve took several deep breaths, and Pine could have sworn he smelled smoke. Perhaps the manacles couldn't fully block his nature, but letting off smoke wouldn't get them very far.

Neve smacked her hand against the wall once, then twice, then a third time.

She tilted her head back and let out a frustrated scream before hitting the wall again.

When she pulled her hand back, there were dark scorch marks on the whitewashed stone.

Pine froze.

Neve didn't seem to notice. She kept beating at the stone as if she could pummel it to bits, but all she would do was beat her hands bloody. He watched for a moment and noticed wisps of smoke coming from her fingers.

He wasn't the one letting off smoke. She was.

But Neve was human. She was from Earth. And while he was no expert on humans, he was fairly confident they couldn't create fire like dragons could.

The only way a human could do that was if she were his mate.

The world seemed to shift under Pine's feet, and he thought of their ride together. There were moments where he was almost certain he'd heard her speaking in his mind, but he'd convinced himself it was impossible. He was either imagining it, or she'd spoken out loud. She couldn't be his mate.

But she was on the verge of summoning fire.

Neve lowered her hands and stepped away from the wall. "You're looking at me like that because I'm going crazy, aren't you?"

He crossed the room and took her hands in his, the manacles around his wrists clanking and making him strain a bit against the weight. Now was not the time for declarations of love or explanations, but he had to make Neve understand. "I think you can get us out of here."

Neve was skeptical. "Me?"

Pine nodded to the scorch marks. "You did that."

Neve followed his gaze and pursed her lips before turning from him and raising a hand to trace over the marks. A bit of soot came away on her finger. She looked at her palm. "My hands are clean. It's not dirt."

"No, it's not." Pine still felt unsteady and couldn't quite believe it. But he had to talk her through this, had to get them out of here. "You summoned some of my fire."

"What?"

"There's a bond between us. It's rare, but it's the only explanation—unless you've been hiding the fact that one of your parents is a dragon." He offered a small smile.

She laughed at that. "My parents are definitely human. One hundred percent." She was still looking at her hands. "How do I do it?"

How could he explain something that was as easy as clenching his fist to someone who'd never consciously done it before? He'd never discussed the mating bond with anyone who had a human mate. He knew Prince Crux had his human mate, Courtney, but asking the details of their bond would have been far too personal.

Now Pine wished he'd been nosy.

He had to say something. "Reach for the power within you, or within me, I guess, and imagine it in your hand. It can't hurt you. A dragon's fire can't harm his mate."

"Mate?" Her eyes widened, and she blinked a few times, her mouth silently forming the word. "You ... me ..." She took a deep breath. "We're going to have a discussion when this all is over."

She closed her eyes and held her palm up, flexing her fingers so they looked like they were holding something large. She strained, face contorted and hand vibrating with the effort to summon his flame. Smoke rose from her fingertips, and Pine held his breath. She could do this. She could get them out of this.

Neve sighed and lowered her hand. "Nothing."

"Not nothing; you were so close." He wanted to take her hand and guide her through this, but he feared the manacles would block whatever power she had. "Try again."

She opened her mouth to say something, possibly to argue, but closed it and held her hand back out. She strained so hard she looked like she might hurt herself.

Nothing happened.

"Toro could come back here any minute," Pine warned. "He's going to drag me before the king and accuse me of treason. It's a capital offense."

"I know that!" Neve scowled. But smoke started to rise from her palm.

Pine kept going. "He'll come for Briar too. And you. He's a thorough bastard. If we don't get out of here before he's ready, we're as good as—"

Neve let out a cry, and fire appeared on her palm. She flexed her fingers and almost closed her hand but flattened it out at the last moment. "Holy shit."

Indeed.

Neve held her arm out in front of her like the flame might engulf her if she brought it too close. "Holy shit. I made fire. What the hell am I supposed to do with it?"

Pine smiled. "Get us out of here."

15

M ate.

The word blared in Neve's mind as she and Pine raced through the halls of the palace to find someone who could untangle this mess.

"Why weren't there guards at the door?" she panted out, trying to focus on the task at hand and not the huge *thing* hanging over their future.

If they had a future.

"Because Toro is using his own hired men. He can't just station them on guard inside the palace. He's already taking a risk by bringing them here at all. If the king doesn't believe his accusations, this will end poorly for him." Pine didn't sound at all out of breath even though they'd been sprinting through the halls for several minutes. Toro may have brought hired help, but that didn't mean they could risk being seen. He had to have allies.

"Do you think the king is going to believe him?" Worry and hope warred inside of her.

Pine's jaw clenched as they rounded another corner. "I don't know. The king has never taken issue with my family, but Toro is cunning. He wouldn't have made his move unless he thought he could succeed."

Fear threatened to make Neve's heart explode. The sapphire grew heavier against her chest with each step, a reminder of what she and Pine might have if they made it out of this alive.

"We need to find Briar," Pine said, slowing his pace to peer down an intersecting hallway. "She should have been a spy, the way she knows things. She'll know who we can trust."

A commotion erupted from somewhere nearby —shouts and the clatter of armor. Pine grabbed Neve's hand and pulled her into an alcove behind a thick tapestry. They pressed close together, chests barely rising as footsteps thundered past.

"Lord Toro wants them found immediately!"

When the voices faded, Neve let out a shaky breath. "Looks like we found his men."

Pine peered out from behind the tapestry, scanning the now-empty hallway. "We need to keep moving."

Neve nodded. As they slipped out of their hiding spot, she caught sight of her reflection in a nearby mirror. Her hair was disheveled, her makeup smudged, and the beautiful gown Pine had given her was wrinkled and torn at the hem. She barely recognized herself.

"This way," Pine whispered, tugging her hand gently. They moved swiftly and quietly, every shadow hiding a potential threat.

As they turned a corner, Neve nearly collided with someone. She stifled a scream, stumbling backward into Pine's chest.

"There you are!" Briar hissed, her eyes wide with relief and worry. "I've been looking everywhere for you two!"

Pine's sister wasn't alone. Beside her stood a tall, imposing man with dark hair and piercing eyes. He radiated an aura of authority that made Neve want to curtsy or something.

"Prince Crux," Pine said, inclining his head slightly. Then he looked to his sister. "Briar?"

"Crux found me after Toro had you arrested. He didn't believe a word of it. He wants to help."

The prince nodded. "Toro finally took this too far. We need to get to my father before he does. If Father makes a declaration about treason before the court, he won't be able to easily take it back. But he hasn't done that yet. There's still time."

Pine held up his manacled hands. "Any idea how to get these off?"

Crux and Briar both studied them. Briar pursed her lips before removing a sturdy pin from her hair. "I got this."

Neve watched Briar pick the lock for a moment, then switched her gaze to Pine's face. He was clearly wondering where his sister had learned that trick, but there wasn't any time to dwell on it.

The manacles fell away, and they hid them under a tapestry.

"Come on," said Crux. "We need to hurry."

Neve thought she and Pine were running before, but Crux had them basically sprinting through the halls and up stairways, twisting through the palace with the knowledge only someone who'd lived there could have. The finally ran out of stairs and ended at a large expanse of rooftop where an imposing figure stood staring out at the vista that lay before him.

King Venin.

He turned as the four of them appeared. "What

are you doing?" he asked Crux. "You know I do not wish to be disturbed when I'm up here."

Crux bowed. So did Pine and Briar. It took a beat, but Neve followed suit. She'd never had to bow to anyone before. It felt strange.

"I am sorry, Father. Things have gone awry at the celebration, and this needs your attention now." Crux stood, but Pine and Briar stayed bent over, so Neve stayed where she was.

The king let out a frustrated sigh. "What is it now?"

"Lord Toro," was all Crux had to say.

Pine and Briar straightened, so Neve did too and just in time to see the king's face turn a disturbing shade of red. Was he going to have a stroke? Could dragons have strokes?

The king made a gesture for Crux to continue talking.

He did. "He's accusing Lord Pine of treason. He's leveled accusations at Lord Pine's father—"

Pine made a sound of outrage then clamped his mouth shut.

"Ridiculous," said the king.

"Yes," Crux continued. "My sources tell me that Toro has run up debts, and he's become desperate. He plans to reveal all to you once you enter the New

Year's Ceremony. He had Pine apprehended in the middle of a dance."

King Venin rested his head in his hand. "Desperate indeed." He looked at Pine. "We have been monitoring Toro for some time. It is unfortunate that you were caught up in this, but I assure you, the kingdom knows that you are loyal."

Something loosened in Neve's chest. Relief. That was it.

The king's words eased some of the tension in the air. Neve saw Pine relax slightly beside her, though his posture remained alert. Briar had a small smile on her face.

"Thank you, Your Majesty," Pine said, bowing his head.

Before the king could make any more declarations, footsteps pounded up the stone steps to the rooftop. Lord Toro strode out, flanked by two guards. His face was a mask of righteous indignation, with just a hint of panic in his eyes.

"Your Majesty!" Toro exclaimed, then faltered as he took in the scene before him. His gaze darted between Pine, Neve, and Crux before settling on the king. "I ... I came to inform you of a grave matter. I request a private audience."

The king made a gesture, inviting him to speak. "This is as private as you'll get, Lord Toro."

Toro hesitated, looking at Pine and noticing the lack of manacles on his hands. He looked back to the king. Then back to Pine.

Would he back down?

The game was over. Everyone knew it. Toro had lost. Maybe if he walked away, he could salvage some of his dignity.

Instead, he summoned a fireball and threw it straight for Pine.

16

Pine threw up a wall of deflecting fire as Toro's flames shot his way. He pushed Neve and Briar aside, desperate to stay between them and danger.

His mate and his sister. Everyone he loved. He would not let Toro destroy them.

Their flames collided in midair, making a spectacular show of heat and light that momentarily blinded everyone on the rooftop.

"Stand down, Toro!" King Venin roared, his voice carrying the weight of his authority.

But Toro was beyond reason. His eyes were wild as he launched another volley of fireballs, this time aiming not just at Pine, but at everyone present.

Including the king.

Fool.

Pine leapt forward, meeting Toro's assault with his own barrage of flames. Fire danced around them. The heat was intense, but Pine barely noticed it, his focus solely on protection.

"Enough of this!" the king shouted, striding forward. "You dare attack a royal in his own palace?"

"I attack a traitor," Toro snarled. More flames roared towards Pine. There was only one way to defend everyone, even if it was against the law to shift form in front of the king without permission.

He let the change wash over him, shifting from man to beast in the space of a breath.

He grew and shifted, stretching out into his dragon form. Wings unfurled, claws dug into the stone. Pine roared, showing Toro the full extent of his power.

And then, he charged.

Toro leapt to meet him, shifting in midair. Their bodies slammed together in a tangle of scales and teeth and flame. Pine's claws sank into the softer underside of Toro's neck, drawing blood.

But Toro was strong. He twisted in Pine's grasp, lashing out with his tail. Pine let go, dancing out of range.

They stared at each other for a long moment, hovering in the air and weighing their options.

Pine didn't want to kill Toro. He might have been trained as a soldier, but he'd never killed anyone before. But if he had to do it to protect his mate, he wouldn't hesitate.

Toro growled, low and dangerous. Then, he lunged, talons extended.

Pine met him in the air, grappling with him. He flew backwards, avoiding Toro's teeth, then he reached for the other dragon's wing. He gripped it firmly, pulling and twisting.

There was a sickening snap, and Toro screamed in pain.

He plummeted from the sky, hitting the ground below them with a crash that sent up a cloud of dust and debris.

Party goers rushed out of the ballroom to gawk at the injured dragon, then—almost as one—they looked up to see Pine in the air. Cries of alarm went up even as the king's guards rushed to circle Toro.

Pine retreated and dropped to the rooftop, shifting back to his other form and bowing before the king, not daring to move.

He wanted to look up and make sure that Neve and Briar were alright, but he feared that even a flinch might be seen as an act of aggression. The king could execute him for shifting shape and fighting with Toro.

"Rise, Lord Pine," the king's voice boomed out over the rooftop.

Pine rose.

The king surveyed him with a steady look. "You have done me a great service today, young lord. Go and enjoy the rest of the party. I think you have a bright future."

The king had demanded that they enjoy the party, but Neve wasn't surprised when Pine tugged on her arm an hour or so later, and they snuck out to catch their carriage and head home.

What a night.

Treason.

Fights.

A mate.

Her mind was in a whirl. All of Toro's plot had taken less than an hour to fall apart, but Neve was still shaking on the inside, sure everything might come crashing down if she looked away from Pine for more than a minute.

They didn't speak. She couldn't think of where to start.

Had Pine suspected the plot?

Had he known she was his mate?

Was she still supposed to go home?

Everything within her rebelled at the thought of leaving him behind. But how could she stay? Sure, she didn't have the most exciting life back home, but she couldn't just leave it behind.

And it wasn't like she could ask him to go with her.

They ended up in Pine's quarters. Neve had been sleeping in there every night, and it was beginning to feel just as much like her room as his. She wanted to sink into the mattress and never move again, but she was still on edge.

She'd controlled fire. How the hell was that even possible?

"Is Lord Toro dead?" It was just about the last thing she cared about, but she needed to break through the silence.

"No," Pine said. He shrugged out of his jacket and draped it over the back of a chair. "He'll live to see the king's justice."

"And what's that going to be?"

"Banishment, most likely. He won't trouble us again." Pine sat at the edge of his large bed.

Neve slipped out of her shoes and sat beside him. "Now would be a good time to explain that whole mate thing." She held her hand out, palm up, and summoned his fire. It was easier now than it had been when they were locked up together, almost like the fire was her own.

Pine let his hand hover above the flames, and they didn't seem to bother him at all. She closed her fist and extinguished the flame.

"My fire cannot harm you. Your fire cannot harm me. When I'm in my dragon form, we can speak mind to mind. We are bound by fate."

"Did you know when we met?" She thought back to every moment of the past few weeks, from the disastrous meeting to the brief first kiss, their fight at the Yule Ball, and then all of those wonderful nights together. Had Pine been keeping this from her the whole time?

"I swear to you I didn't."

There was more to say, so much more, but exhaustion was pulling hard at Neve, and she couldn't stop the yawn that tore out of her mouth. Pine wrapped an arm around her shoulders, and she leaned into him.

"Sleep," he said. "We're safe. I'll keep you safe."

Even though she was still in her dress, the softness of the mattress and the warmth of his embrace was too much, and Neve slept.

17

Neve woke alone.

It wasn't the first time, though she'd awoken in Pine's embrace more mornings than not in the past weeks. She took off the gown from the night before but hesitated to take off the necklace. She smoothed her hand over the chain and left it in place. It was expensive, and she didn't want to just leave it laying out in Pine's room.

The room she'd been given had a closet full of gorgeous clothes she'd been given since arriving, but her suitcase with her things from Earth was at the foot of the bed, and she slipped on a comfortable pair of pants and one of her favorite tops. It felt a little like armor. She let the necklace sit right against her skin instead of pulling it out to lay on the shirt.

She wasn't hiding it, but the feel of the metal against her skin was a reminder that Pine had given it to her.

Or maybe she was beginning to crave gems. Did dragons actually have hoards, or was that another dragon fact she'd have to unlearn?

Pine wasn't in the breakfast room or any other place in the manor that she looked. That's when she started to worry.

Has last night been too much for him?

She'd been consumed by wondering if she'd reached her breaking point that she hadn't considered that he could have reached his.

I'll keep you safe.

Those words had sounded like a vow as she drifted to sleep, but now she wasn't so sure.

Maybe Pine was out flying. If she were a dragon, she'd take to the skies every time she needed to clear her head.

She put on a coat and headed out, walking the same way they'd gone for their second flight. It was a little warmer than it had been over the last two weeks, so her skin didn't feel like it was being picked at with an axe, but it was still chilly. When she tilted her head up to take in the sky, she didn't see any dragons.

What she did see were footsteps in the snow leading to a large building. She recognized it; it was where she'd first arrived. It had seemed farther away then.

She followed the footsteps to the door and let herself in, some instinct telling her that it was where she needed to be.

She found Pine standing on the ramp to what had to be a small spaceship, though it was about the size of a commercial airplane. He was hauling a large crate into the ship. When he turned around and saw her, he froze.

"Are ... are you sending me home?" It was their agreement. She knew that going into this. She wouldn't have stayed if he hadn't promised. But she'd thought something had changed last night.

Was she wrong?

A look of horror washed over Pine's face, and he rushed off the ramp, crossing the hangar to her and grasping her hands in his. "Is that what you want?" The words sounded torn out of his throat.

She had a whole life back on Earth she was supposed to want. Parents, a job, a decent apartment. She kept meaning to pick up some kind of hobby, even if it hadn't happened yet. Asking to stay meant never seeing her parents again. Sure, they were a bit self-absorbed. But skipping their Christmas party didn't mean she wanted to cut off all contact forever.

But if she had to choose between them and Pine?

She barely knew him. They'd been together less than two weeks.

He was her mate.

When she opened her mouth, words refused to come out.

Pine cupped her cheek and captured her lips with his own. She fell into the kiss, grateful to surrender, for the reprieve. "I don't want to leave you." The words tumbled out as they separated. "But I can't just abandon everything, can I? We barely—"

Pine kissed her again, softly this time, and then pulled back, smiling. "I didn't sleep much last night," he admitted.

"And ..." She'd fallen asleep in his arms and slept like the dead. Had he been lying there awake for hours?

"And I thought now might be the perfect time to take a trip, to see the galaxy, that sort of thing. But for some places, I might need a guide."

She tried to suppress the smile threatening to bloom, and it didn't work. "Like where?"

"I hear there's this fascinating place called Earth. Did you know they don't even have dragons there?" He was grinning.

"We do have dragons," she countered. "They just don't turn into devilishly handsome lords."

"So you think I'm handsome?"

"You're something."

"You are the most beautiful woman I've ever met, and I want to spend my life with you. What do you say?"

Neve smiled. "When do we leave?" She wrapped her arms around him tightly and kissed him with everything she had. She wasn't letting her dragon lord go.

Thank you for reading Pine!

I'd appreciate it so much if you would consider leaving a review.

The Detyen Warrior Outcasts series will continue.

NEED MORE OUT OF THIS WORLD ROMANCE?

Sign up at the link below to **keep in touch and you'll get a free ebook!**

Get your freebie!
https://signup.katerudolph.net/subscribe

Looking for EVEN MORE alien romance?

Prince Crux is in a bind.

When the Dragon King commands Crux find a mate, his days of carefree bachelorhood are over. One trip to a psychic matchmaker and he's on the path to his destiny. But it all comes screeching to a halt when he meets a human woman who lights his inner fire and makes him yearn.

She's got a pair of roller skates and an attitude.

Courtney is supposed to be putting the shambles of her life back together. Getting abducted by aliens isn't part of the plan. Neither is getting rescued by a scorchingly hot dragon that makes her think of an impossible future. But they have no chance together if they can't first escape a planet full of monsters intent on their destruction.

Get your copy of Crux

https://shop.katerudolph.net/products/crux

WHAT TO READ NEXT: CRUX

Prince Crux is in a bind.

When the Dragon King commands Crux find a mate, his days of carefree bachelorhood are over. One trip to a psychic matchmaker and he's on the path to his destiny. But it all comes screeching to a halt when he meets a human woman who lights his inner fire and makes him yearn.

She's got a pair of roller skates and an attitude.

Courtney is supposed to be putting the shambles of her life back together. Getting abducted by aliens isn't part of the plan. Neither is getting rescued by a scorchingly hot dragon that makes her think of an impossible future. But they have no chance together if they can't first escape a planet full of monsters intent on their destruction.

Courtney Lamb's feet were heavy, and she had the headache to end all headaches. She curled into herself on one side, trying to scrunch up into a ball, but her feet dragged along the floor and noise echoed off the metal walls around her.

She was still wearing her roller skates.

How? She always took them off before leaving work. She couldn't exactly drive with wheels on her feet. And yet, as she turned over and pulled her legs in, they slipped on the cold metal floor.

Where was she? This wasn't the root beer stand she worked at, nor was it the creepy, decrepit steel barn that sat on the very edge of the restaurant property. She looked around, squinting in the dim light and trying to get her bearings.

It was industrial, but the room was small. Steel walls. No windows. And a weird echo-y noise in the distance that might have been an air conditioner.

She didn't see a door.

Courtney scrambled to her knees before realizing she wasn't going to get far with roller skates on her feet. She shucked the skates off and wiggled her toes in her sweaty socks before tying the laces together. No matter what was going on, she didn't want to lose her skates.

They were expensive. And one of the few nice things she had left.

There was a shriek down the hall, or at least, Courtney assumed there was a hall, and she flinched.

What the hell was going on?

Had she been kidnapped? Was she being trafficked? She'd seen plenty of Facebook posts talking about the perils of being a woman in America, but most of it seemed like a bunch of bullshit. People didn't *actually* hide under cars to slit the Achilles tendons of the unsuspecting.

Right?

She ran a hand down the back of her leg, as if to

assure herself that she was intact. Obviously she was. Other than the headache, she wasn't hurt.

She was just confused.

And in trouble.

She wanted to call for help, but a second scream from somewhere in the building made her throat freeze up. No, she didn't want to call attention to herself.

With her skate laces tied together, she was able to sling her skates over her shoulder and get to her feet. The room seemed even tinier when she was standing up. Was she a prisoner? Why?

Her mom was going to kill her when she found out.

Of course, Courtney hadn't spoken to her mother in months, and now was not the time to think about how this would impact her mother's career. She was in the middle of an abduction, she had to care about herself.

She stroked the top of her skate, half for comfort, half to remind herself that it was sturdy and could probably be used as some kind of weapon.

She was wearing the thick leggings and short sleeve red tunic that made up her work uniform, though her name badge must have fallen off somewhere. That furthered Courtney's theory that she'd been taken from work.

She couldn't remember clocking out. She wracked her brain, but the last thing she remembered was telling her co-worker, Sarah, that she didn't have any plans for the weekend. The same as every weekend these days.

That wasn't what she should be feeling bad about at the moment.

Was Sarah a trafficker? Had she waited to strike until Courtney was at her most vulnerable?

No. That was ridiculous. Sarah was a college student trying to make ends meet. She wasn't sinister.

Where was the freaking door?

Courtney whirled around, but she still didn't see anything that looked like it would let her out of the room. She was in a metal tomb and she couldn't escape.

Her breaths came faster and faster, and black spots danced in front of her eyes.

No. No. Now was not the time for a panic attack.

She hadn't had one in months, and she didn't want them to restart. They sucked.

And so did her whole situation.

"Think of the good things," she commanded

herself. There weren't many. But she had to number them off. "I'm in my regular clothes. My skates are fine. I'm not hurt." She ran out of optimism after that. Any other "good" news sounded like asking for trouble, and Courtney wasn't interested in that.

She ran her hands over the metal walls, looking for a seam that might reveal a hidden door. There had to be something. She had been put in the room, so there had to be a way to get her out of it. She looked up, wondering if she'd somehow been lowered in, but the ceiling was too high to make out any fine detail in the dim light.

Where was the light even coming from?

There wasn't a ceiling light. She didn't see lights in the floor. There was just a faint, pale blue glow all around her that allowed her to see.

It was another good thing, and Courtney decided not to question it.

She had her skates, but she wished she had a skate tool. That fancy little wrench might have helped her pry an invisible door open. But her skate tool and spare wheels were in her bag at work. Along with her cell phone, a bit of cash, and her car keys. She had no way to contact anyone for help.

And *there* was the hyperventilation.

She tried to control her breathing, but the walls

felt like they were closing in. She heard footsteps coming her way and shrank back as far away from the sound as she could. The room was maybe six feet wide. She couldn't shrink back much.

A brave woman would have done something. Courtney *wished* she was brave. But she couldn't think and she wanted to live. She was pretty sure brave people died quicker than cowards.

The wall opposite her glowed a faint yellow, and a rectangle formed before sliding to one side, the invisible door revealing itself. A brave woman would have charged.

Instead, Courtney watched a monster step inside.

It—and it was clearly an *it*, not a person—was some kind of *creature*. Over eight feet tall, antennae coming out of its head, and sinister purple skin that was covered in a faint slime. It wore clothes over most of its body, but its arms were exposed, and scars or tattoos or something covered it.

One of its hands wasn't a hand at all. Instead, it came to a fine point and had an edge that made it look like a sword.

It looked like something out of *Star Trek*.

And she was wearing a red shirt.

Shit.

It wore pants, but judging by the giant bulge right where his dick should be, he didn't plan on wearing them for long. And she didn't want to find out if his dick was a knife too.

Working by instinct, not pausing to think, Courtney grabbed onto one of her skates and swung, sending the other one flying at the monster's head. He didn't expect it, and the wheels, metal plate, and carbon fiber boot were enough to send him slumping to the ground.

Oh god, was he dead? Had she broken her skate?

Courtney flailed for a moment and cut off the horrible noise that tried to escape her throat. She checked her skate first. Except for a bit of slime and something that might have been monster blood, it seemed fine.

Good.

She didn't know how to check for a pulse on a monster. She didn't know if she wanted him to be dead or alive.

Oh god. What was she going to do?

She had to run.

She stepped around the monster and dove through the door, just in case it tried to close. The hallway was narrow and lit up by the same ambient blue light as her cell. She chose a direction and ran, unsure if it was correct but refusing to hesitate.

She stumbled when she passed a window.

Courtney came to a halt and looked outside.

She expected a city. Maybe some trees. *Something*.

Instead, she saw the black of space.

Outer space.

She wasn't in a warehouse. She was on a space ship, and they were hovering above some planet that didn't look like Earth.

How was she going to get home?

She was trying to think, then something impacted the ship, and Courtney stumbled as the lights went out and all of her senses went haywire.

INTERGALACTIC DATING AGENCY

Looking for love that's out of this world? These strong, smart, sexy aliens are seeking mates from the Milky Way. Just hop onboard with your local Intergalactic Dating Agency. Join our group of authors as we explore the friendly skies and beyond with trilogies of cosmic craving, astral adventure, and otherworldly lovers. Warning: abductions may or may not be included!

ALSO BY KATE RUDOLPH

Dragon Brides
Dragon Princes. Fierce Women. Love.
Fated mates, fierce women, and dragon princes are ready to find their mates.

Crux

Ranger

Saber

Cipher

Storm

Drake

Asher

Knox

Flint

Pine

Guarded by the Shifter

Werewolf. Bodyguard. Mate.

The origins of these shifters are shrouded in mystery, but they're determined to protect their mates from any harm that comes their way.

Also available in audio!

Hunting Season
On the Prowl
Stalking Magic
Hungry for the Wolf
Wolf Cursed (novella)
Wolf's Temptation

Stealing the Alpha

The thief takes what she wants, but the alpha keeps what's his...

Join shifter thief Mel as she clashes with lion alpha Luke in an explosive trilogy of two opposites who can't keep away from one another.

Also available in audio!

The Alpha Heist
Entangled with the Thief
In the Alpha's Bed

Alien Mates: Planet Exile

Guerran is no place for pretty human women. But these alien heroes will protect their mates!
Also available in audio!

Exile's Hunter
Exile's Adored

Zulir Warrior Mates

Kidnapped humans. Alien Warriors. Electric wings.
The Zulir Warrior Mates series brings you human heroines and heroes abducted from Earth who find love – and wings! – with the alien warriors who rescue them.
Also available in audio!

Synnr's Saint
Synnr's Hope
Synnr's Spark
Synnr's Kiss
Synnr's Ride

Mated to the Alien

Fated Mate Alien Romance

Detyens are doomed to die young if they don't find their fated mates.

Follow along as these mated pairs fight off aliens, corrupt dictators, prejudiced humans, pirates, and more! The books can be read or listened to in any order, though some characters show up in multiple stories.

Select books available in audio.

Pick a book and jump into the action today!

Ruwen
Tyral
Stoan
Cyborg
Krayter
Kayleb

Shayn

Braxtyn

Doryan

Dekon

Detyen Warriors

Detya was destroyed a hundred years ago. These doomed warriors are out to find justice... and their mates.

The Detyen Warriors series brings you kick butt heroines, alpha alien heroes, fated mates, and relationships strong enough to span the galaxy!

The entire series is also available in audio!

Soulless

Ruthless

Heartless

Faultless

Endless

Detyen Warrior Outcasts
Fated Mate Alien Romance

These doomed warriors were abandoned by their people and live on the edge. Their mates hold the key to their salvation.
Pick a book and jump into the action today!

Dangerous Bond
Intrepid Bond
Wayward Bond

Alien Holiday Romance

Christmas... in space????
These alien holiday romances look beyond Earth's winter holidays and ring in the season across the galaxy!
Select titles available in audio.
Snowed in with the Alien Beast
The Alien's Winter Gift
The Alien Reindeer's Wild Ride
Trapped with her Alien Mate

Alien Outlaws

Outlaws, schemes, and love... it's all there in the Alien Outlaws series...

Andie Munster is sick of life on Ixilta, the planet she got dumped on after being abducted from Earth six years ago. And when the mysterious and dangerous Xandr shows up looking for a way off the planet, she's half-prisoner, half-co-conspirator in a wild rush to escape.

Rogue Alien's Escape
Rogue Alien's Woman
Rogue Alien's Secret
Rogue Alien's Legacy

Find more by Kate Rudolph at www. katerudolph.net

ABOUT KATE RUDOLPH

Kate Rudolph is a paranormal and sci-fi romance writer who lives in Indiana. She loves writing about kick butt heroines and the steamy heroes who love them. She's been devouring romance novels since she was too young to be reading them and had to hide her books so no one would take them away. She couldn't imagine a better job in this world than writing romances and sharing them with her fellow readers.

If you enjoyed this story, please consider leaving a review.